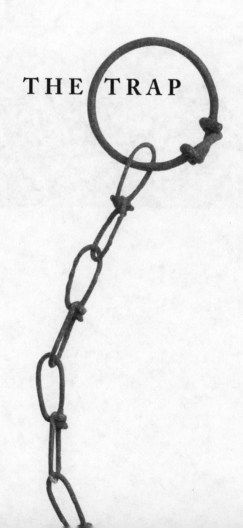

THE TRAP

john smelcer

THE TRAP

HENRY HOLT AND COMPANY

SQUARE
FISH

For Herbert Smelcer, beloved uncle

*The author would like to thank Bard Young, Rod Clark, Pamela Smelcer,
Catherine Creger, James Welch, and Laura Godwin for their editorial comments,
and the James Jones Literary Society for selecting this novel as the winner
of the 2004 James Jones First Novel Fellowship.*

**SQUARE
FISH**

An Imprint of Holtzbrinck Publishers

Excerpts from these chapters have previously appeared in the following:
chapters 2 in *Talkeetna Good Times;* 3 in *Rosebud;* 4 in *Provincetown Arts.*

Library of Congress Cataloging-in-Publication Data
Smelcer, John E. / The trap / John Smelcer.—1st ed.   p.   cm.
Summary: In alternating chapters, seventeen-year-old Johnny Least-
Weasel, who is better known for brains than brawn, worries about his
missing grandfather, and the grandfather, Albert Least-Weasel, struggles
to survive, caught in his own steel trap in the Alaskan winter.
[1. Survival—Fiction.   2. Conduct of life—Fiction.   3. Trapping—
Fiction.   4. Old age—Fiction.   5. Indians of North America—
Alaska—Fiction.   6. Alaska—Fiction.]   I. Title.
PZ7.S6397Tra 2006   [Fic]—dc22   2005035740

ISBN-13: 978-0-312-37755-7 / ISBN-10: 0-312-37755-X

Originally published in the United States by Henry Holt and Company
Designed by Meredith Pratt
Square Fish logo designed by Filomena Tuosto

10 9 8 7 6 5
www.squarefishbooks.com

THE FIRST DAY

▼

Back before white men were searching for gold in the hills and streams of this North Country, there was a village much like any other small village nestled along the great river. One fall, several young men went moose hunting. A man asked if he could join them, even though he was very old and slow. Reluctantly, the young men let him come along.

OFF IN THE DISTANCE, in a place far away from any-place else, a yellow snowmobile pulling a long sled was slowly coming down toward the wide river through a valley of white hills, winding around trees, traversing over knolls and rises, sometimes becom-ing visible, sometimes moving unseen. The sun was already at its highest point, which was barely above the rim of the blue-edged horizon. That's the way it had been for the past month and the way it would be for at least another month to come. Winter this far north was a series of short days and long nights, with mostly cold and silence in between—a time when most living things huddled or slept through the intolerable cold and dark.

It had snowed during the night, which, like the prolonged darkness, was nothing new. It always snowed here, more so in the mountains, and the wind swept the whiteness against trees and deadfalls and the steep banks of streams or lakes. To escape the pitiless wind, sled dogs learned to dig down into the snow and to curl up into tight balls with their long, bushy tails covering their noses and eyes like fur quilts. They'd sleep that way all night, cold and dreaming of summer and sunlight warm upon them.

Sometimes the snow buried sleeping moose or cabins, drifted over backcountry trails, and concealed treacherous openings in the great river far below, the river that wound itself through the floodplain to the sea.

They say the People of the North have a hundred names for snow. This may not be completely true, but anyone who has lived any time on a frozen land knows that snow has more than one name.

There is sleet, and hail so big around that the sound of it falling on a tin roof is deafening. There are dry, soft flakes that fall gently without hurry or anger, like the lazy flakes in a Christmas-card scene. There is wet snow that sticks to the branches of trees, turns to ice, and breaks their limbs when too much has gathered. Some snow falls straight down, some slant-wise, and some from everywhere, even from beneath, as if the freezing earth itself is storming. There is powder snow, which, when loosely settled on a field or valley, creates an almost religious experience for those fortunate enough to be the first to break trails, leaving their long, unbroken signatures on the snow-clad landscape.

Sometimes, when conditions are right, there is granulated snow, like sugar, loosely packed and crys-talline, which gives teeth to the wind. After a very cold night, when the cold pulls out all moisture from the air, there is dry snow. On a warm winter day, a rare day, the low sun melts only the thinnest layer of snow closest to the surface and then refreezes it at night. This is crusted snow. After a trail is broken into the backcountry, the next morning there will be packed snow, hard and unyielding—a narrow road through the wilderness used by man and animal alike.

In high winds, when little snow is falling, the wind can sweep up snow from fields, shake it loose from trees, and swirl it about the world like a blender. This is a flurry. Add a great deal of new snow and you have a blizzard—so dense the earth and sky seem to merge into one whiteness.

In late spring, when the sun hangs on the horizon longer and longer each day, there can be slush, more water than ice.

Only the foolish would say there is one word for snow. Anything that lasts so long and buries a world must be many-named.

Rounding the last turn, disappearing for a minute and then coming into view again, the snowmobile dragged itself and its sled up to a stand of trees and stopped. For an instant, the only sound in the hills was the gentle push of a breeze and the groan of a man rising from the machine.

He stood and looked out across the great land that his ancestors had lived on since the beginning. How long, he did not know. No one knew. But he knew this was his land. Every single place had a name. The names were ancient, and sometimes no one could remember what they meant or why, but that did not matter. The land had always known its place. The names given to it by man only comforted man. They mattered not at all to the hills or the far white mountains, the quiet river below or the large tree in its winter sleep, gently swaying and creaking in the wind.

When he stepped from the machine, he sank almost to his waist in snow. It was loose, the way snow is in the first hours after it falls, before it has time to change its mind and become something else. With his teeth, he pulled off his sealskin gloves, which fell and hung loosely, one at each hip because they were tied together across the shoulders of his parka.

The sun was so low it reflected off the icy crystals of snow, nearly blinding the man who held a naked hand against his forehead and slowly turned to look out across the world. Small clouds of breath billowed and faded as cold began to settle in his fingers.

He squinted hard and for a long time watched and listened. The sky was dark blue and contrasted against the blanketed white of the earth. It was a beautiful place, lovely and deadly all at once, a land of great power. Its voice seemed to ring out from its highest mountains, to be carried by the wind off glaciers down toward the sea, and to say that it could kill you in a second. Those who perish here cannot hear the voice to heed its warning.

Most men have become deaf. They can barely hear each other anymore, much less nature's whisperings. Nature is not tailored to man. It exists for itself.

After a few minutes, the man turned toward the trees, pulled off his brown fur hat, and placed it on the black seat of the machine. The seat was cracked in a few places, and the back part was entirely covered in gray duct tape. The machine and the man had covered many miles together. He was old, with fairly long dark hair and only a whisper of a black mustache. A shadow of a rough beard was just beginning to grow, black and gray, salt and pepper, the stubble from a few days without a razor. His face was weathered, and deep lines ran across it like the ever-changing channels of the river in the valley below. It wasn't a face forged simply by age, but a face that had been exposed too long in a land where time is measured not by the slow ticking hands of clocks, but by the quiet changing of seasons. It was a face weathered by erosion, like canyons or deserts.

The old man looked at something hanging from one of the lowest branches of a tree, a rabbit dangling from a string tied around one leg. It was frozen rigid and swayed slightly in the breeze pouring down from the mountains, across the hills, and out across the flats where villages nestled along the wide river's edge. He could see that it was whole, that no animal had tried to pull it down from the tree.

He had strung it up a few days earlier as bait to trap fox or wolverine, lynx or wolf. At the base of the tree, secured by a rusted chain bolted to it, he had placed a steel trap, its sharp teeth spread apart and open in wait for a paw to step on it, for the furred weight to trigger a latch that would send the metal teeth crushing into flesh and bone.

He had set such traps under trees all along the two branches of his trapline, each some twenty miles long from beginning to end. He would set them a mile apart, hang the rabbit, and return in a few days to see what had been drawn in by the scent. Most of the time, there would be nothing but the rabbit, but sometimes there would be another animal. Sometimes it was still alive and its leg would be bleeding, the snow red all around the trap, and, in some cases much of the paw would be chewed away in the animal's attempt to break free. Sometimes the animal was already dead and frozen stiff, having fallen victim to the cold.

All up and down the valley and the surrounding hills, such traps were set, their springs tight, their teeth sharpened, waiting patiently like winter, with neither memory nor regret.

This is how he had done it all his life. This is how his father had taught him. It was the way of the trapper, part of life and death in these white rolling hills.

Underneath the swaying rabbit, the perfect snow was undisturbed except for an almost imperceptible trail of a shrew, which had run across the snow beneath the tree, stopped here and there, and then turned back on itself before disappearing into a small hole.

The wind lifted the man's hair and blew it into his eyes. He swiped it away and trudged the few yards to his sled, where he untied a pair of snowshoes and pulled a short flat-head shovel from alongside the runners.

Strapped into the belly of the metal-framed cargo sled were two frozen quarters of a moose, each weighing over a hundred pounds. The man had shot it the day before near one of his trapping cabins. Now it accompanied him on his journey home. The rest of the moose meat was hanging from the rafters inside the cabin so that animals could not get to it. It would stay frozen inside the small log house, and the old man would come back in a few days or a week to haul it home on the same sled. That was one good thing about the long deep freeze of winter.

A strong white cord crisscrossed over the quarters and through the sled's frame to hold them down during the bumpy journey. On top of the meat, held down tight by black rubber cords, was an old army knapsack stuffed with those things important to surviving winter on this land. There was a hatchet, a dented old pot blackened from years of hanging over small camp-fires, utensils, a metal cup, a handsaw, extra dry socks, matches, toilet paper, and food—unsalted dry biscuits called pilot crackers, a half-filled container of oat-meal, dry salmon strips, jerky, salt and pepper, and always a can of Spam and a jar of dark instant coffee.

It was the kind of pack anyone who knew this country would carry out into the wilderness. The pack was a common thing, like carrying an extra five gallons of gas on snowmobile or boat trips between the river villages.

The man carried the snowshoes and the shovel over to the still-hot snowmobile and jabbed them into the snow so that they stood almost straight up, casting long shadows down the trail. He sat on the seat and pulled a piece of jerky out from somewhere inside his fur-trimmed parka. As he tugged with his teeth at the dried meat, he looked around and smiled. His teeth were white and strong, perhaps wider than most, but there were few cavities for such a broad smile. He smiled because he was home. He was always home in this country. This place was where he had lived out the many years of his life and where he would one day die and be buried in the small cemetery on the hill overlooking his village and the great river.

They say it is enough for animals to know existence. But for Indians, they must also marvel at it. Perhaps that is the difference between them.

Albert Least-Weasel sat eating his jerky and watching the white world for a long time, smiling and squinting at the bright landscape. When he finished eating, he grabbed the short wooden-handled shovel and tossed it toward the tree and the trap. It landed close to the tree, but not too close, and stuck upright, its worn and faded handle looking like a thin grayish tree with no limbs. He would use the shovel to remove snow from around the base of the tree so that the trap would be exposed, free to show its teeth and shine in the sunlight.

The old man trudged through the deep snow until he was almost under the dead rabbit swinging stiffly in the breeze. He looked at it closely. Its white fur was ragged and full of holes where camprobbers—small, intelligent light-gray birds of the north, had pecked at it. Perhaps a raven may have been at it as well. It was hard to tell the difference. The old man cut the string tied to the rabbit's hind leg with his single-blade pocketknife and tossed the carcass far away. He would set fresh bait above the trap, a long piece of moose meat laced with brown hair and sinew. But first he would clear the area beneath the tree and check to see if the trap was still set.

The old man always placed his traps directly under the bait, so he was careful not to stand too close to where the trap lay beneath the soft new snow.

He studied the snow. It wasn't all that deep. The great boughs of the tree protected the base so that only a portion of snow had filtered down to the ground beneath. The snow was not even up to his knees, while out on the field a dozen yards away it was almost waist-deep. He wouldn't need the shovel. Instead, standing close to the tree with one hand firmly set against its trunk, he kicked away the snow using the flat side of his boot and leg, the way an ice fisherman clears snow above the lid of a frozen lake. Before long, he had cleared away much of the snow, except for the area directly under where the frozen bait had hung.

It wasn't really hard work, but he grew tired quickly and stopped to catch his breath. He was hot from the labor and unzipped his parka until the metal teeth let go of each other and the parka swung open like a tent door. Albert stood beneath the tree for a few minutes until his heart slowed down and he felt cool.

He was almost eighty. The years had been catching up with him, not slowly like the ticking second hands of his old wind-up wristwatch, but in great leaps like spawning salmon jumping waterfalls.

When he was ready, he turned back to the task of removing snow with his boots. Again, he placed one hand on the tree to steady himself and kicked until he could see the frozen moss and grass underneath the snow. He was working his way out from the base of the tree when it happened. There was a soft click as the teeth of steel closed on his leg. The foot or so of snow covering the trap may have slowed its speed. The snow must have muffled the sound too, because he didn't recall hearing it when it clamped down on his leg. This was a sensation he had never felt before. He had always wondered about a moment like this. A moment he had assigned to the suffering of others but never to himself. The steel of his own trap now gripped his right leg—but not as quickly or as sharply as he would have imagined. In fact, it didn't really hurt all that much. It was more a tightness, like when the doctor who flew into his village took his blood pressure. The way his arm felt when the doctor pumped up the black band.

For the first time in his life, Albert understood what an animal must feel, what every animal he had ever trapped must have felt.

The old man raised his foot to see with his eye what he saw in his mind. When he did, the chain pulled itself out of the snow and drew a straight line from the man to the tree trunk only a few feet away. With his foot off the ground, he could see how the steel teeth had closed only an inch or so above the knob of his ankle. There was no blood. The sharp teeth had penetrated the thin brown leather of his boot but not the thick lining or his wool socks that kept his feet warm even to thirty or forty below.

With the low sun so near light's last breaking, skimming on the bulging edge of the world, Albert Least-Weasel put his foot down and laughed. His situation wasn't really a funny thing, but it wasn't as bad as it could have been, more irritating than dangerous. He would simply remove the trap, reset it, and be on his way home, where by late evening he would sit beside a crackling woodstove with his wife, sipping hot black tea and eating moose-nose soup with hardtack for his supper.

From the far side of the wide field came the soft hoot of an owl.

A long time ago, all the men in a small village along the sea wanted to be warriors. Each morning they ran down to the sea and jumped into the freezing water. They stayed in the water until they almost froze to death, thereby proving their strength. Afterward, they beat one another with branches to learn endurance of pain and to toughen their skin. They all wrestled and boasted of their strength. Then they took turns trying to pull a great tree from the ground. Try as they might, none could tear the tree from its roots.

A YOUNG MAN quickly closed the cabin door and leaned against it with all his weight to make sure that it was shut tight. He was around seventeen, tall and lean, with long black hair hanging halfway to his waist. It was warm inside the small log house, and he didn't want the warm air with its smell of wood smoke to escape. When he was sure that he had secured the door, he took off his parka, fur hat, and gloves and laid everything on a wooden crate full of split wood sitting near the rattling black woodstove. He could tell from listening that the stove was burning too hot and too fast, so he turned the threaded damper a few turns until, nearly starved for air, the fire settled down and fell upon itself. Soon, the split birch logs whispered only to each other, the way they were supposed to, once the heavy iron door was closed.

Johnny Least-Weasel had helped his grandfather to fell the trees upriver in the summer, to cut them into six-foot lengths, which they left to dry along the banks until the river froze. When the ice was thick enough, they hauled the logs home on long hand-made sleds pulled behind snowmobiles. All of the homes in the village were heated by firewood. Oil cost too much to ship this far north. Besides, the great land had always provided for their needs.

An old woman was sitting on a couch, sewing slow stitches into a moccasin, one of a pair made of tanned moose leather. It was brown and trimmed with beaver, and she was sewing onto its top a floral pattern made of very small red and white and green beads. She had not made the pattern, because the beadwork was far too delicate and intricate for her hands now. Besides, she could not see so closely any longer. The old woman had traded dried salmon strips for the patterns, and now the moccasins would be presents for her children and their children. It was something they all came to expect at Christmas—handmade moccasins and thick wool socks ordered from the Sears catalog. Both would be either two sizes too large or two sizes too small, but they kept them nonetheless because they loved the old woman.

"Johnny," she said without looking up from her work, "did you get the water like I asked?"

"Yes, Grandma," the young man said while lifting the lid to a large pot on the propane cooking stove.

The soup was boiling too high, so he turned it down as he had done to the fire. The soup stopped rolling, and he stirred it with a long metal spoon.

"What are we having, Grandma?" he asked without turning.

"Caribou soup. I put an onion and some carrots and potatoes in it. It should be done." She was still sewing the colorful pattern onto the soft tongue of the moccasin.

The young man stood by the fire for a minute and then went outside to the snowmobile and pulled two blue five-gallon plastic jugs from a metal sled. With one in each hand, each weighing some forty pounds, he carried them into the cabin and set them on the kitchen floor. Then he placed one on top of the counter, and the other he set in the corner to the left of the stove on which the hot pot of simmering soup sat.

"Thank you, Johnny," the old woman said as she set her needlework aside and got up to check the soup and take bowls and spoons from the cupboard. She moved slowly, the way people who have lived for a very long time always move, as if every muscle was stiff and ached. She had long gray hair, though in fact it was more silver than gray.

Johnny Least-Weasel helped his grandmother. He always had. That was his father's way and the way his grandfather had taught his father. That was the way of his people, of all Indian people. Here, the old were respected for many reasons, not just because they knew about the old ways. They were respected as much for having survived in a world so hostile that the phrase in their language for greeting someone meant "So, you're still alive."

"Respect the elders," they had always said. "Help them out."

When he caught a great many salmon in his fish trap, Johnny always gave the biggest and best fish to the elders who no longer fished or hunted for themselves. And when he was lucky and shot a moose or caribou, he offered them whichever parts they wanted. They always asked for the liver and the heart. When he shot a moose, they asked for the nose to make moose-nose soup.

They also made soup from king-salmon heads. After cutting the head off just before the gills, they slit the head longways, from the nose holes straight back, so that the head lies in two perfect wedges. While exposed, the two halves of the brain, small as grains of sand, are clearly visible.

There is a story that, in the beginning, salmon could not swim down to the river bottom because they had air in their heads that made them float back to the surface, where they were easy prey for eagles and bears. The chief of the Salmon People complained to Raven, who opened their heads and put two small rocks inside so that they could sink to the safety of the depths. Since that time, all salmon can swim deep, and when you cut their heads in half, you can still see the two tiny rocks Raven put there.

Back when the old woman was young, Indians would wait one day after catching salmon before they would cut them up so that the salmon's spirits could have time to leave their bodies. Nowadays, when Indians caught salmon, they didn't wait so long, but they still tossed the skeletons back into the river so that the spirits could return to that place where all Salmon People live. In this northland, the connection to nature was not yet fully broken.

Recently the old woman had become more and more forgetful, less aware, increasingly dependent on the familiarity of the small tilted cabin. During the previous fall, she had asked her grandson to take her berry picking. On the way, Johnny had seen a herd of caribou swimming across a small lake—their antlered heads just above the waterline. He crept down to the edge, hiding behind a stand of willow. There were four of them coming directly at him, and they would soon stand on the shore. Kneeling, he raised his rifle, aimed at the closest animal, and waited. Just as he was about to pull the trigger, his grandmother walked up beside him, standing where the surprised caribou could see her clearly.

"What are you doing, Johnny?" she asked.

Seeing her, the small herd turned and swam away toward the far side of the lake, and quickly vanished into the forest.

The old woman shuffled around the kitchen while her grandson set the table. He tossed the empty and half-empty cans of soda into the garbage and wiped the tabletop in tight circles with a rag. Before they sat down, he turned the old black-and-white television set so that they could see it from the table while they ate.

The house boasted a main room, which included a kitchen area, a dining table with only two chairs that did not match, and a little additional space for sitting. Two kerosene lamps lit the space in a soft, warm light. A door at the back led to the tiny bedroom.

There was no bathroom. No one in the village had a real bathroom. Instead, they had outhouses and honey pots for when the need came late at night, when it was too dark or too cold to go outside.

Framed pictures and a stretched black bearskin rug hung on the wall, and a cross hung above the couch. The wood floor was bare and rubbed smooth in places. The entire cabin was slightly tilted from settling. Every year, the permafrost heaved and shifted the house up or down, this way or that way. But it was a comfortable house. Not a particularly good house, but it had stood in this place for more than fifty years, and it was always warm inside, and the smell of coffee always greeted visitors at the door.

The young man could tell that the woodstove was barely breathing, so he opened the damper a tiny bit, just enough until he could hear the fire catch again, the flames coming back from their hiding place deep inside the logs. The Indian knew the secret of wood. He knew that all trees held fire deep in their hearts, somewhere near the core. Great Raven had put it there in the time of long ago to give Indians warmth. And any single tree had only so much heat to give.

That was the law of things. Let it burn too quickly and it would be gone quickly. The trick was to bring out the flames slowly, at just the right height, so that the heat could last for hours. In this country, where fire means life, it took skill and years of experience with wood and the ax to bring out the flames and to make them last through the long nights of winter.

Warmth was so precious in the far north that men went to great lengths to trap it. All log cabins, even the very-best-made ones, suffered from crevices and cracks where the hewn logs did not fit perfectly. Into such spaces people pushed moss to keep heat from escaping. They called this chinking. It took hours to heat up even a small log cabin, but once done, once the logs themselves had absorbed the warmth through-out their entire length, to the core, they would stay warm for half a day after the fire had died and embers had turned to ash.

Without fire, no one would survive January or February, when it is so cold that nothing moves. When even the propane that feeds the lights and the cook-ing stove wants to remain motionless, waiting until the sun warms the metal skin of the tank.

Outside the cabin, all along an entire wall, ran a stack of firewood as tall as the old woman and two sticks deep, except for a gap in the first several yards of the line. The wood had already been hauled inside, tossed into its crate, and later fed to the hungry woodstove that never slept and always rattled while it was burning. Although it never went outside, the stove knew that the wood was there, waiting.

Johnny and his grandmother talked very little while they ate. Now and then, the gas lights flickered and a piece of firewood in the stove popped.

Peering out the large window in the front wall of the cabin, Johnny watched a raven sitting on a tree. It sat on a limb, its keen black eyes searching for food on the ground. Finding nothing, it flew away, low over the treetops, until Johnny could no longer see it. The bird reminded him of the many stories his grandparents had told him about Raven. His favorites were the ones about how Raven made the world and about the time he stole the stars, the moon, and the sun from an old chief so that there would be light in the world.

"Grandma," the young man said, still looking out the window.

The old woman looked up from her soup, wiped her mouth, gazed at her grandson but said nothing.

There was a commercial for new Cadillacs on the television.

"When will Grandpa be back from his trapline?" he asked.

"Hmm," she said in more of a grunt than a word. "I don't know for sure. When we were young and I was skinny and pretty, he stayed for only a few days. But after so many years, he stays longer sometimes. If the hunting is good and he catches lots of wolves and fox or shoots a moose or caribou, he stays longer. If the weather is good, he maybe stay for a few more days. It depends on the weather, I guess."

When the old woman was first married, she had accompanied her husband and his friends on a moose hunt. It was late fall and the forest was leafless and gray. The crisp air smelled of rotting leaves and berries. One morning, after an early breakfast, the men left to search upriver for moose. Morrie stayed behind in the warm cabin.

"Hunting," her husband had told her as he shoved

the long green boat from the sandy shore, "is the work of men."

But shortly after they left—the faraway sound of the outboard still echoing in the hills—a large bull moose stepped out from the naked forest surrounding the cabin and stood beside the woodpile. Morrie took her rifle, left for her protection in the event of bears, and killed it with her first shot. She spent the rest of the day cleaning the old cabin, sweeping the floor, splitting firewood and kindling, and slow-cooking a pot of stew made with fresh meat from a hindquarter of the moose.

When the men returned after dark—hungry, tired, cold, and empty-handed—they were surprised to see that the woman had done what they had not. They were shamed. At first they were silent, but they couldn't hold back their tongues. Halfway through their supper of moose stew, each man in turn began to praise the woman hunter. Morrie was embarrassed and said nothing for a while. But as the men continued to praise her, she eventually began to laugh. Soon, everyone was laughing and joking about the day. Someone even said she would make a "good man."

They still talked about it.

She looked out the window, saw the sun already going to the other side of the world for the night, and then she turned her attention back to her bowl of soup.

"I wish I had gone with him this time," Johnny said, reaching for a piece of bread to dip in his soup.

"Hmm," the old woman said again. "He happy by himself."

Johnny thought about her words for a moment before he spoke again.

"But I worry about him. Sometimes I dream he gets hurt, or that his snowmobile won't start or runs out of gas and that he's stuck way out there alone," he said, nodding toward the window as he uttered the last words of his sentence.

Morrie Least-Weasel spoke slowly, the way all elders did. She was born before there were many white people in their country, back when all Indians still spoke Indian.

"He been going out there to that trapline since before you daddy born. He don't need you or nobody when he go out there. Someday you learn that, Johnny."

The old woman smiled, and finished her last spoonful, but there was something in her voice and the way she looked at the outside thermometer and the clearing sky that bothered him. It was as if she, too, was concerned, but respected her husband's pride enough not to send the boy after him when he was not yet gone too long. While vision and hearing fades, old bones turn thin and brittle, and once-strong muscles grow weak, pride endures to the very end—resisting change like the great land itself.

People say that wild animals—bears and wolves—held in captivity die not from a lack of food or water or from disease, but from a loss of pride.

Now the television show they had been watching was on again. It was about a group of teenagers who lived in Beverly Hills. The characters were sitting and talking over espresso in a huge mall with more stores in it than salmon in a river in July. The young people in the villages watched the show and talked about it. They wanted fast cars; swimming pools; bright, crowded shopping malls; and cell phones buzzing in their ears like mosquitoes.

But they could have none of that here. Not one

part. Most of the teens had never even been beyond the next few villages up or down the great river. They knew, vaguely, that a whole other world existed far beyond the white mountains in the direction where the sun arose each morning. But they watched the TV show every week just like they went to church on Sunday, where they learned that Raven was really a skinny white man with long hair, blue eyes, and a beard, a man whom no one had loved enough to save when he was nailed to a totem pole.

The old woman didn't care for it—the television show. She stood up, took her bowl and spoon over to the sink, and poured some coffee into a white cup with "INDIAN PRIDE" printed in bright red letters on it.

"Want some, Johnny?" she asked, lifting the old-style percolator pot.

"Yes, *tsin'aen*," he said, and brought over a cup with the symbol of their tribe on the side. *Tsin'aen* was their word for "thank you," and he pronounced it "chen-nen." He knew some words that his grandparents had taught him, mostly the names of animals and how to count to ten, but only the elders still spoke the language. Apparently it was a secret you could not know until you had lived for a very long time.

When he finished his coffee, Johnny placed his cup and bowl and spoon in the sink and turned off the television. He opened the latch to the woodstove, saw that there was only a glowing bed of red embers, and stuffed two fat pieces of wood into it before closing its door and spinning the damper open until he could hear the glowing embers bite into the bottom log, find its secret place, and drag its flames screaming and hissing into the world.

He watched the fire for a few minutes, turned down the damper, and put on his parka, hat, and gloves. He stopped at the door and turned to the old woman sitting on the couch with her moccasins and needle.

"Good night, Grandma. I'll stop in and see you tomorrow."

"You a good boy, Johnny," she replied, looking up only briefly.

With that, he opened the door and stepped into the thick, swallowing darkness. It was so dark that it seemed as though some of the light went out of the cabin and was replaced by grayness. He closed the door, pulling hard until he heard the lock catch, and then he walked out into the frozen world, pulled the starter rope of his snowmobile twice, and drove back toward the village set along the great river's edge. His dim yellowish headlight bounced off trees and snow-banks and the occasional rabbit as he made his way below bright and luminous stars.

When they were far up in the hills, the hunters saw a grizzly bear coming slowly toward them. It was the biggest bear they had ever seen. The young men started yelling and throwing rocks and shooting arrows at the bear, which only made it angry. All the young men ran away, leaving the old man to face the giant bear alone.

THE TINY SHREW that had made the faint, scurrying tracks in the new snow darted from its hole and disappeared around the back side of the tree. A slight breeze brought the scent of spruce down through the swaying dark green boughs, settling on the old man at its base.

Albert Least-Weasel knelt on one knee on the hard frozen earth he had uncovered and studied the trap. The metal was very cold, and it burned his fingers when he touched it. A few degrees colder and his skin would have stuck to the trap.

But Albert knew better than to touch the metal in a situation like that, so he pulled his gloves back over his freezing hands.

All traps such as this one work in the same way. The hunter steps on both sides until his weight opens the snarling teeth. Then, still standing, he reaches down between the straining jaws and sets a small, thin latch that holds the teeth wide open. The bigger the trap, the more weight it takes to pull open the hungry teeth.

A grizzly trap took two men to set. Even then, it was a scary thing to do.

Albert Least-Weasel remembered what happened to a man from a village downriver, about thirty years before. Maybe longer. The man and his cousin were setting grizzly traps in a cluster all around a tree. There must have been about six or seven traps, maybe more, and they hung a whole moose front-quarter from a strong branch about eight feet off the ground. When he was done hoisting the heavy bait, the man accidentally backed up and stepped into one of the monstrous contraptions. When the steel jaws closed, they shattered his leg bone about a foot above his ankle, and the man from downriver fell backward into the waiting jaws of another grizzly trap, which killed him instantly.

The old man hadn't set such a dangerous trap since the death of his own father many years ago. Many bears used to roam these hills, especially in late summer when they'd comb the hillsides for ripe berries before descending to the river to eat spawned salmon rotting on the banks and shores.

There weren't as many bears anymore. There weren't as many of a lot of things nowadays. Villagers had to travel farther and farther from home to find big game.

With his one foot inside the trap, even though it didn't hurt, Albert could not press down on the two sides evenly with enough weight or pressure to open the persistent jaws. He tried pushing down on each side with all his weight on his gloved hands, feeling the strain through his arms and shoulders, but the trap would not open. Not even a little. It just glared up at him as the sun shone off the snow. It knew nothing except that it was closed as it had been a hundred times, and that it was happy to be closed, to be relieved of the tension of the springs.

The old man slowly stood up, stretched, and placed both hands on the small of his back while he looked around and listened.

It was quiet, except for the wind, but he could hear the voice of the land talking to him. It always talked to him, telling him when to put on a jacket or take his boat out of the water. It told him when to push his fish trap into the silty river and when to put his snowmobile away for the winter.

It spoke to him now.

But he did not like what it had to say. It said something about old age and forgetfulness. It said something about endings, the way it must have talked to every animal ever caught in a trap.

This time, the man placed his free foot on the trap and put all his weight on the one side, but again it didn't open. It was a good trap, a sharp-toothed trap with a good strong spring. He had picked it just because of this, because he wanted his trap to be strong, and now it would not open even though he wanted it to.

Albert tried opening the trap several times, but with each attempt it only stared back at him. The trap was a stupid thing. It didn't care what it caught, just so that it caught something. It just sat there, grinning without lips. Only teeth.

For the first time, the old man began to worry.

He was far from home, and there would be no one around for many miles. This was his trapline, as it had been for most of his life. The villagers respected this knowledge and stayed away so as not to frighten game. It was one of the unwritten rules among the people of the north. His cabins had been broken into only once in the past twenty years, and the break-in had been the doing of white hunters who'd flown in on a small aircraft during a winter caribou hunt.

Looking west, he saw that the sun was already so low on the edge of the world that it would be dark soon. With the darkness would come the cold.

It had been fairly warm for several days, close to zero, maybe a few degrees above or below. But the clouds, which usually bring warmth, like a pillowy layer of white and gray insulation, had been thinning, moving out. Soon, it would get colder.

Albert Least-Weasel knew it meant trouble if he couldn't free himself soon. But he wasn't afraid. It was true that he was named for a clever and ferocious small animal that eats nearly half its own body weight daily, but it was also true that he was named after a great chief from the Gulkana River region: Chief Least-Weasel Cuuy. There is a saying in Indian about that old chief. They say, *"Cuuy yen su xona c'aa delyaa- gen su'adelniinen,"* which means, "It is said that remarkable things happened to Chief Cuuy."

As Albert stood there thinking about his predica- ment, he saw the handle of his shovel sticking upright in the snow where it had landed. It came to him then that he could use the flat metal blade to pry open the trap.

He shuffled around the tree as far as the bolted chain allowed, and reached for the handle. But it was too far away from his hand by more than a body length. The old man was not distracted and did not pause. Instead, he found a branch lying on the ground, broke off the smaller limbs, and used the long stick to try to pull the handle back toward him. He thought that if he could hook the handle near the top and pull slowly, the shovel would fall backward, toward him, bringing it closer by a few feet. Then, he'd simply use the stick to drag it closer.

But when he reached out as far as his hand could extend with the stick, he accidentally pushed the top of the gray wooden handle, and the shovel fell forward, away from the tree. When it landed, much of it was buried under the soft new snow. Albert Least-Weasel spent the next half hour, well into darkness, trying to hook the metal blade to drag the shovel closer, but it never hooked, and it never moved. It just lay there taunting him as if it did not exist at all, as if it were still strapped on the back of the sled.

This distressed him. There, only a dozen long steps away, was his snowmobile with his gear, even an ax with which he could cut out the deep bolt holding the chain to the tree trunk. Also, there on the sled was his rifle, a sleeping bag, and some food and coffee.

Everything he needed to survive the night was on that sled, but, chained as he was, it might as well have been a thousand miles away.

He wanted a cup of hot coffee right then. He could almost smell it.

The sun was gone now. For the next eighteen or nineteen hours, it would be only an insistent memory to the animals who lived on this land. Even the unthinking mountains and the river in the valley far below would wait for it. Bears were smart enough to curl up and sleep through the long winter months when there would be too little to eat and too much darkness.

The old man would miss the sun the most.

He gave up trying to get the shovel. He knew that he needed to think about other things. He could return to the shovel in the morning. For now, he would prepare for the quickly coming, long-staying, intolerable night.

Least-Weasel knew he needed to get his body off the frozen ground. Even inside a tent, a sleeping bag must not touch the frozen earth, which can pull out all a body's heat, just as metal can steal the warmth from fingertips, hands, or tongue.

Knowing this, knowing such things about life in the north, Albert broke off some of the spruce tree's green boughs, which hung from all about his head and grew out far from the tree's trunk, like the frame of an umbrella. Some of the lower branches were as thin as a finger, long and wispy. But most were as thick as the man's wrist. He worked up a sweat trying to break them down, and after a while he had enough to build a small, thick bed on which to lie huddled. He collected all the smaller pieces, even those that had fallen down naturally from the wind and lay scattered about the ground beneath the tree, to build a small fire, using the pack of matches inside his shirt pocket.

He always carried matches on such trips. Sometimes he would arrive at one of his small trapping cabins just after light abandoned the land, and he used to fumble around looking for matches in the cabin to light the oil lamps, the candles, and the small wood-stove. By carrying matches with him, he avoided the fumbling and bumping into things.

Besides, sometimes he liked to stop along the trail to build a small fire for making coffee or for companionship.

He built a little fire, more to comfort than to warm him. The wind was dying down for the night, which was a good thing. The man kept the fire alive by feeding thin, kindling-sized pieces of wood to the yellow flames. He knew that if he built too big a fire, his fuel would be consumed too quickly, leaving him with nothing before the night was far spent. So he kept it small and huddled close.

While staring into the flames, listening to the wood crackling as it burned, he remembered an old story about the first fire. It was a story he had heard and told many times in his long life. It is said that, a very long time ago, Indians did not have fire. They sat around in the dark eating meat raw, and they were always cold during the eternal winters. But Great Raven took pity on them as they huddled in the darkness freezing, so he asked the animals to give Man fire. Several animals tried to bring a firebrand from the rim of a volcano, but only Owl was able to carry the burning branch. He carried it in his beak, which used to be very long. But the firebrand burned down his beak until there was only a little bit left. They say that is why owls have such short beaks nowadays.

The old man also remembered a saying about how Indians build small fires and stay close, while white men build great big fires with gasoline and whole logs but stand very far away so as not to get burned. Surely, he thought, something in that saying spoke truly of the two peoples' philosophy of nature and its resources.

Under a veil of stars with only a slight breeze fanning the boughs of the tree and the small yellow flames of the fire, the old man turned toward his village, toward home. For more than fifty years, whenever he was away from his wife while hunting or trapping, he would turn toward home and sing a love song to her in their Indian language. It was a sad love song, and it was the only song he ever sang to her; and although she never heard the words drifting over the great expanses or falling down valleys like rain, she always stopped whatever she was doing just as the sun set on the far horizon and hummed the same sad little song.

When he had finished singing, Least-Weasel lay on his bed of piled spruce boughs, and he was glad for his fur hat, his gloves, and his warm boots. But he knew that if the temperature went down, none of these things would help him for long. Many times in his life he had slept outdoors without fear or question.

But this time was different and he knew it.

Tired and nervous, he carefully placed a few more pieces of wood onto the tight flames about two feet from his face and said a small prayer for all things living. Just before he fell asleep, fitfully, somewhere from up in the hills, below where the moon rested on the knifed edge of the dark world—clean and white, as if it were chiseled from the sky—wolves began to howl, followed by a long, hard silence.

The chief of the village had a nephew named Blackskin. The young man did not go down to stand in the sea or try to lift the great tree as the other men did. Instead, he stayed in the village and helped the elders. He brought them water and cut firewood to keep their fires burning. He slept by the fire and his skin was black from the ash and soot. The other men thought he was weak and lazy and they made fun of him. They didn't know that every night Blackskin went down to the icy sea and stayed in longer than any of them, and he lifted great rocks over his head.

AFTER DRIVING THE THREE MILES between his grandparents' cabin and the small, sleepy village, Johnny Least-Weasel turned from the main trail that ran along the river and stopped his snowmobile in front of a cabin where several other machines were already parked in the yard. The log house looked like many of the other cabins in the village—snow-beaten and weathered—driven into the ground by the heavy loads of too many winters.

A dozen sled dogs barked from the roofs of their small plywood houses until they saw who it was, recognized the figure, then settled down and curled back upon themselves. Two ravens, ubiquitous black birds of the north, were pecking at garbage scattered on the ground beside a torn dark green plastic bag. In many northern cultures, the raven, because of his tenacity and keen intelligence, was viewed as a deity of sorts—part creator, part destroyer—always the famished trickster.

Ravens may be among the most intelligent of creatures. Ice fishermen have seen them wait in nearby trees until the stout fishing rods begin to bounce up and down, a sure sign that a fish is hooked, and then swoop down and pull the line up, a foot at a time, with their strong black beaks, stepping on the line each time to hold it fast. They repeat this until the wiggling fish is pulled from the hole—ample reward for their problem-solving ability.

Johnny had once watched a dozen ravens steal scraps from a wolf trying to protect his meal. While the others stayed a safe distance, one raven grabbed the wolf's tail and yanked it until the annoyed canine turned and chased him into the forest, momentarily abandoning his prize to the murder of ravens that quickly fell upon it.

When he was fourteen, Johnny had witnessed a very strange sight—something no one but his grandfather believed. But it was true nonetheless. He had come upon a small wintry field full of ravens. There must have been more than a hundred. Every tree held a dozen birds, little black-robed priests, staring at the center of the field where a dead raven lay on the snow.

It was a funeral. A raven funeral.

They were mourning, cawing and cawing until, as if by some unvoiced signal, they stopped and flew away, leaving Johnny standing alone in the gathering silence of their wake.

And no one in the village, or in any nearby village, had ever seen a raven nest or hatchling. It was almost as if their presence in the far northland was by magic. And yet they were as ubiquitous as the changing seasons. It was no wonder the raven had become a central character in the myths belonging to Johnny's people.

The two birds stopped rummaging, looked up, and cawed at the man. It was a warning to stay away.

The cabin lights were all on, and Johnny could hear loud country music and talking and laughing coming from inside. Smoke was rising from the chimney, so he knew that the cabin was warm, and sparks were pouring into the night sky as well, like the first stars Raven stole from a chief in the old stories. This meant the fire was breathing too much.

Although it had been cloudy during the past several days, the sky was clearing and he could see stars through the holes in the low clouds. When he walked toward the cabin, he could hear and feel the snow crunching the way it did when it was cold and dry. Sometimes, you can tell the humidity and temperature outside just by the way snow feels and sounds beneath your boots.

Johnny knew from the way the treetops swayed and the low clouds above them slid quickly overhead that the sky would continue to clear and that the temperature would probably drop ten or twenty degrees.

He walked up the creaking steps, took off his hat

and gloves, knocked the snow from his boots, and stepped inside.

The room was full of Indians. That's what Indians call themselves, not Native Americans or American Indians. He recognized lots of people he knew. Everyone knew everyone in the village, and most of them were related. That closeness was comfortable, but it had drawbacks, too. For one thing, young people had to go to other villages to find suitable husbands or wives.

His uncle was sitting at a table piled with empty bottles, ashtrays, and beer cans. Three other Indians sat with him.

"Johnny!" his uncle yelled across the small cabin. "Where you been?"

The stereo, an eight-track player hooked up to a car battery, was too loud, and Johnny could barely hear him. People sat around the room in old wooden chairs, and someone was sleeping on the red couch. None of the furniture matched. Everyone was drinking beer or whiskey and smoking cigarettes. The room was full of smoke and the smell of wood burning.

"I was at Grandma's," he said, leaning close to his uncle so that he could be heard over the din. "She needed me to haul some water and bring in some firewood."

His uncle smiled and patted his nephew on the shoulder.

"Good for you!" he said and then laughed. "Pour yourself a drink. There's some glasses and ice on the counter."

Johnny didn't drink anymore and his uncle knew it. Among all his friends, he was the only one who didn't.

"I'm okay," he replied, looking down at the painted plywood floor. "I'm not thirsty."

One of the other men called across the room.

"Hey, Johnny! Get me a beer!" The man was only a few years older than he, maybe twenty. His eyes were glassy. "They're outside on the porch," he said, pointing toward the door. Someone else yelled from across the room to bring him one too. It was Peter Johns, who had gone to school with Least-Weasel all of his life.

Johnny went outside, took two beers from an open

case, brought them inside, and gave them to the two men, who did not thank him.

It had always been this way. The other young men in the village saw Johnny's polite kindness as a weakness, and made fun of him—everyone, that is, except his grandfather, who knew that Johnny was becoming a good man, a strong man, the way men used to be back when there were few white people in this country, back when Indians still lived the old way, close to nature, and closer still to one another. People relied on one another. Their myths were full of stories about the rewards of kindness and giving, about how the strong helped the weak and how the young helped the old.

One of Johnny's favorites was a story of how a great Indian warrior once helped a small mouse with a berry in its mouth, struggling over a log. The Indian helped the mouse, and that winter when his people were starving, the mouse returned the favor by providing the man with a packsack full of dry berries and fish, saving the village. Many of the myths the elders told were about compassion, something the world seemed to be missing nowadays.

Johnny walked past his uncle, who grabbed him by the shirtsleeve and held up his empty glass, shaking it so that the ice cubes rattled. It was his way of asking for a refill.

The young Indian took the glass, dropped in a handful of ice cubes, and poured only a tiny bit of whiskey before filling the glass with cola and stirring it. He tasted it. It was weak, but he knew that after so many glasses, his uncle could no longer tell the difference. It was his way of helping his uncle, whom he loved very much.

In the years since his father had left, Johnny had lived on and off with his mother, who drank too much and blamed him for his father's absence; with his uncle; or with his grandparents, in whose cabin he slept uncomfortably on a tired old sofa. But for much of the past year Johnny had lived in his own small cabin next door to his uncle's.

Sometimes, running low on booze, his uncle gave him money and told him to take his snowmobile up to the liquor store to buy a half gallon of cheap whiskey. And although Johnny was not old enough, he would go but always came back with a small pint and told his uncle that the store was out of the larger bottles. Though it was a trick, Johnny suspected that his uncle knew what he was trying to do.

Sometimes, when it was only the two of them, he and his uncle would go out very late at night, stand in the thick darkness, and shout to the far mountains. It was more song than shout. They'd sing and dance to the mountains, calling to the ancestors whose spirits dwell there.

Hai hai! Hai hai!

They say that the plumes of smoke from volcanic vents are the campfires of ancestors long dead. His uncle always tried to teach Johnny the old ways.

"How's Grandpa?" his uncle asked, even though it was his own father he asked about.

"He's not home. He went up his trapline a few days ago. Grandma thinks he'll come home tomorrow."

Finishing the last of his drink, his uncle looked concerned and angry.

"He's too old to go hunting by himself. Everyone knows that. He needs to stay home like all the other old men."

From across the room, Peter Johns joined in the conversation.

"Yeah!" he shouted to Johnny's uncle, who owned the cabin and the booze. "That old man should stay home! He's way too old! Trapping in winter is for young men!"

Johnny looked at his uncle and spoke softly. "He'll be all right. He's been doing it all his life."

Peter drained his glass before replying.

"Maybe he has, but he's getting too old for it now. He has no business out there anymore."

"He'll be okay. He'll be home tomorrow," Johnny said, his voice lacking conviction.

His uncle held out out his empty glass and rattled it again. The obedient nephew took it.

"Remember what happened last winter?" Peter Johns lit a cigarette. "Your old man got up one night and walked out of his cabin. Just plain walked out. Didn't even take his coat or hat. Nothing. Just walked out in the middle of the night, and we didn't find him until the next morning, three or four miles downriver, talking about going to the sea."

One of the other men sitting at the table joined in the discussion, "That's right. That old man needs help. You shouldn't let him go anywhere by himself."

"It's what makes him happy, I guess," Johnny's uncle said, looking out the window at the thermometer nailed to a spruce tree, then saying nothing again for a long time.

Johnny finished mixing the weak drink and handed it to his uncle.

"He'll be okay," he said, finding his coat where he left it. "I just know it."

That said, the young man pulled his arms through his heavy parka, zipped it closed, and with his hat and gloves in hand, walked out into the night, where he could see more stars than before. He walked away from the light and noise of the cabin and stood on the trail for a long time, listening to the wind and the soft hoot of a far-off owl, watching stars, and thinking about his grandfather. Light from the moon bathed the world so brightly that the space between trees was sharp and clear in the silvery night.

It was getting colder. Johnny pulled the fur-lined

hood of his parka over his head and walked toward his own cabin with the sound of snow crunching beneath his boots.

"He should be back tomorrow," he thought, as a star raced across the sky just below the North Star.

"He should be back tomorrow for sure."

THE SECOND DAY

When it was close, the big bear charged the old man, who had only a walking stick, so he jumped up and down and yelled at the bear, telling it to go away. He shouted these things in his language, which the bear understood because back then bears understood Indians. That bear didn't know what to think, so he just stopped and sat down and shook his great shaggy head.

IT HAD BEEN A LONG NIGHT, and the old man had slept little. Because he fed the fire only thin pieces of wood, the flames never lasted for long. He awoke every hour, added kindling to the shallow bed of faint glowing embers, and gently blew on the base until the fire jumped out of the twigs and eerily shone on the boughs hanging from the great tree just above him. After a while, though, the blaze dropped from the fire and the sphere of light grew smaller until the branches above disappeared.

Sleeping with one leg chained complicated his attempts to rest, and finding a position that was comfortable for more than a few minutes was impossible.

As it did everywhere in the world so close to the Arctic Circle, the sun hugged the trembling horizon as it eventually arose in the east and the short winter day began.

Albert Least-Weasel sat against the tree trunk while he woke up. Too far away, the snowmobile still waited as it had waited all through the darkness, taunting him with its sled of meat and its pack full of the things he needed. This morning, he wanted coffee. Lots of it. Hot and black. He wanted a roaring fire and a pot of coffee sitting on the edge of the fire, boiling away, cheerfully singing its happy little song of percolation.

He remembered the jerky in his pocket, so he took it out from inside his parka. It was as long and thick as his middle finger. Maybe a little bigger. He bit off small pieces and chewed them slowly while thinking about what he must do.

After eating, the old man stood up and stretched. His body ached from the long cold night and from the constant tossing and turning. He rubbed his thighs and arms vigorously for a few minutes until they felt warm from the friction. Then he took off his gloves and rubbed his cheeks.

His visible breath hung in the still air of early morning.

The fire was dead again, so he broke off small pieces of twigs and set them on the coals and blew upon them. It didn't take long until there were flames once more. The old man placed a few larger sticks across the pile and squatted close, warming his hands and face and listening to the popping and hissing of the fire as it ate its breakfast.

Least-Weasel thought of all the campfires he had ever sat around in his life. There must have been thousands. There was always a fire when he spent any time in the forest. Usually, though, he had an ax or a saw or even a chain saw to build much larger fires made from dead timber falls. Around these fires, men would sit and talk all night, telling old hunting stories, myths, family histories, or just talking about the night and the fire. Sometimes, when ice fishing, he built a fire but never stood near it. It was as if having a fire nearby made the wilderness less menacing. It was a powerful thing, something no other animal could make. And it had magic. The shifting colors of the flames and the sound of hissing and popping was mesmerizing. Sometimes, the men just sat quietly for long spells and said absolutely nothing, stared into the flames and listened to its ancient stories.

Least-Weasel was thirsty, but he knew that it was bad to eat snow for water. When it is so cold outside, the body spends so much energy to melt snow into water that the effort is counterproductive. But the snow closest to the fire was already partially melted into a translucent slush. This would be better, so the old man cupped up several handfuls covered with specks of ash from the fire and a few pine needles, and swallowed it. When he was done, he held his hands over the flames to warm them.

Finally warm enough, he stood up and studied his situation. It was obvious what he had to do. Either the trap had to come off his foot, or he had to pull the long bolt out of the tree so that the chain would fall free. He had set the bolt with a hammer and a ratchet wrench, so he knew that it was buried at least six inches into the wood. Maybe more. In summer, pulling the bolt out would have been an easy enough task with a wrench. But now, with the temperatures below zero and with nothing more than a small pocket-knife, it would be more difficult. In such cold, the frozen moisture in the tree might as well be concrete.

The old man grabbed the chain about a foot from the bolt and pulled. He pulled with all his strength, even setting one foot against the tree for leverage. But no matter how sharply he yanked the chain, the stubborn bolt did not move.

Pulling on the chain reminded Least-Weasel of the time his father had caught a great grizzly bear. No one ever actually saw it, but one of the footprints measured about a foot across. The dangerous trap had been attached by a truck-winch cable to a tree, not unlike the great spruce tree above the old man. The cable had a working strength of several thousand pounds. When Albert and his father and uncle returned a few days later, the bear was gone but the earth around the tree looked as if a bulldozer had plowed it, and the bark on the tree trunk was ripped away all around the tree's base. When they were close, they saw that the bear had actually broken the steel cable. There was blood all around and pieces of light brown, almost blond fur. They never found the grizzly.

If the great bear could escape, then so could a man.

Albert Least-Weasel took out his pocketknife. It was an Old Timer, just as he was. He had carried this gift from his father for perhaps forty years. It was thin and had only one blade, which he sharpened and oiled frequently. He pulled open the knife and tried to cut out the bolt. He knew it would be slow and that he had to be careful not to press so hard that he broke the blade, which flexed when he pushed it against the frozen tree.

It didn't take long to remove the bark, but the trunk itself was frozen hard and resistant like steel. After he had cut maybe an inch into the wood, it was clear that he would cut no more. No matter how hard he pushed or what the angle he set the blade, he could remove no more wood from around the bolt. Frustrated, he pressed the knife a little harder, saw it bend more than it had before, and saw it snap in two. The tip of the blade fell to the base of the tree and lay shining on the frozen ground.

The old man leaned against the tree, his head against the trunk and one arm still holding the knife in the hand that hung limply at his side. He was beginning to lose hope.

When he turned around, he could see the handle of his ax sticking out from the sled, its long shadow reaching halfway across the distance in between. The old man thought about how he could use the sharp-edged ax to free himself. With it, he could hack the hard-set bolt free of the tree. But there was another use. Many years ago, his friend Martin Frank was riding a snowmobile in the far backcountry, checking his trapline. His rifle began to slip off the machine, and he grabbed for it. Somehow he caught his hand in the moving rubber tread, which yanked him from the machine, wedging his hand between the tread and the frame and the wheels. Although he struggled desperately, he couldn't free it. He was far from the village, and it was already twenty below zero. It was his own trapline, and he knew that no one would be traveling on it—no one would be coming to help. After waiting for much of a day, Martin rolled up his jacket and shirtsleeve to expose his arm, numbing the area around his wrist with snow, and then, when he thought his wrist ready, he reached for the ax strapped on the back of the snowmobile. With one clean stroke he chopped off his hand and then drove an hour to the nearest cabin for help.

The old man looked at the ax handle. If only he had that, he would have been free yesterday, and today he would be home with his wife inside his warm cabin with the smell of hot coffee and bacon drifting from the stove. He would be wearing his favorite, worn moccasins and shuffling around the small house while his wife knitted or sewed something for the grandchildren. He would be home, and his grandson would come over to help him cut up the two heavy moose quarters and haul more firewood into the house.

But such thoughts did nothing to remove the chain, so the old man brushed them away from his mind.

He did not know how long he would be trapped,

but he knew that someone would come for him soon—
if not today, then the next day, or the next. He had to
survive only until they came upriver from the village
and up into these hills.

Least-Weasel was still hungry. The piece of jerky
had not been enough. Besides, it was the only thing
he had eaten in about eighteen hours. Maybe longer.
He had eaten breakfast the day before, some biscuits
and fried Spam, but he could not remember having
eaten since. If he was to wait until people came to rescue him, he would need food.

A massive pile of empty pinecones had been lying
on the snow all around the tree's base when he'd first
arrived. Clearly, he thought, there were squirrels living in this tree.

The old man slowly unlaced the heavy strings on
the boot caught in the trap. He cut off about six
inches, which he used to tie off the top two eyelets to
keep his boot closed, so that the warmth of his foot
would not escape. The rest he used to tie a loose slip-
knot, similar to a rabbit snare, only smaller. He set the
noose in the branches as far up as he could reach, in a
place where there were many pinecones. He placed it

where the bough was thick and green and where a squirrel might not see it. Once he was certain of its position, he turned away, sat down on his pile of spruce boughs, leaned against the tree, and waited. He waited for the sun to warm the day, for someone to pass by on the trail, for the sound of a squirrel scurrying down the tree.

Having nothing else to do, he set a few pieces of wood onto the fire and waited. But only the wind arrived, tossing the highest boughs back and forth like a shaggy dog shaking off water.

For the time being, the light from the low sun warmed him and he fell asleep. The old man dreamed of long ago, when as a boy he had gone hunting with his uncle. It was fall, before the heavy snow, when the air carries the first small flurries. They call it termination dust because it spells the end of fall. The two had been checking traps all day when they came to the last one. Seeing nothing from the main trail, they stopped to have a snack before the long push home. Young Albert sat on the ground near a tree and waited for his uncle to dig out food from his pack.

While he waited, he loosened the string of one of his boots to remove a pebble lodged between his toes.

Just then, they heard a sound, the rattling of a chain. Albert, one foot lifted off the ground, his boot in his hand, looked over his shoulder and saw, only a few feet away, a snared wolverine, its lips pulled back, its many sharp yellow teeth in full display, its small ears laid back flat, the way many animals show that they are angry and that the people who have angered them are in danger. The chain was strewn behind him, not taut. He was crouched to spring.

The fierce animal jumped at the boy with its shiny dark brown claws splayed far apart, when thunder rang out and the terrible flying creature fell from midair and lay crumpled on the leaf-covered ground. It did not move. When Albert and his uncle went to remove the wolverine from the trap, they saw that it had been caught by only a toe. Surely, his uncle told him, the weight of the jump would have torn it loose, and it would have killed the boy had he not been there to shoot it.

After that, Albert learned to respect the animals he

trapped. He also worked and saved enough money to buy his own rifle. He remembered the day he bought it, how shiny and smooth the cold steel was. It was the possession that inspired the most pride in him, signaling that he was becoming a man. He still owned it, the blue-black metal worn shiny in places, nicks and scratches in the wood stock from years of handling.

The old man slept comfortably for an hour or two before something awakened him. It was the sound of wolves. There were two of them standing by his sled. They were tearing off chunks of the moose, growling and fighting for bits and pieces that fell on the snow. Though they had smelled the meat for a mile, they did not know the man was so close. Sitting as still as he was, quietly sleeping against the tree, they had not seen him.

The man stood up and yelled, waving his arms and shouting. At his first motions, they jumped, surprised, then turned and ran away, each carrying a bit of moose meat as they loped across the wide field and into the trees beyond.

For several minutes after they had vanished into

the trees and hills, the old man's heart still pounded, not from the labor of standing and shouting, but from fear. If the wolves had attacked him, he would have had no means of defending himself. Chained to the tree as he was, he could not have escaped. It was ironic, he thought, that he had set this very trap to catch a wolf, and now here he was, caught in its steel jaws, and it was the wolves who came to see what the trap caught today.

But they might come back. Normally, wolves would not attack a man. But it had been an especially hard winter, too long-lived and harsh, and there had been few caribou or moose. The wolves had passed the miserably cold and dark days chasing field mice and catching an occasional rabbit to fill their tight bellies.

The old man set his mind on escaping. With renewed strength from his peaceful rest, Least-Weasel took the chain in his hands again, pressed his one foot solidly against the trunk just below the bolt, and pulled with all his muscles. He could feel the sharpness of the effort up through his arms, to his shoulders, and around to his back. He held his breath and then repeatedly yanked so hard on the chain that the jolting of the force felt as if someone were beating him on the back and shoulders with an ax handle. But he ignored the pain and pulled and yanked until he was too tired to try again.

Yet the bolt did not move. It was too far into the frozen tree.

He knelt down on one knee as he had done before and tried to press with his gloved hands on the two sides of the trap to open it. Tired as he was from pulling on the chain, nothing moved.

Convinced that he would not escape, he decided to make a weapon to defend himself should the wolves return, drawn in by the scent of fresh meat on the sled. The old man shuffled around the base of the tree, carefully studying those limbs he could reach. Eventually, he found one that was suitable. It was long and straight and just big enough in girth for his first two fingertips to graze his thumb when he wrapped his hand around it. It took him a while to break the branch from the tree, but eventually it snapped loudly and crashed down onto the snow. The old man broke off its smaller branches, which he saved for the fire. Then he held up the straight pole to better measure its length. It was too long, and the tip end was too small around, so he stepped on the pole a few feet from the end and lifted on the other side. Again, the limb snapped, and the short piece fell away.

He threw the tip end onto the fire. It was the biggest piece of wood it had been fed all day.

Least-Weasel held up the stick once more. Now it was about as long as he was tall, but it had a good heft and the tip was still pretty thick. He sat down on his pile of green boughs and sharpened the tip with his broken-bladed knife. When he was done, he held the end over the fire just high enough so that it did not catch and burn. He did this for a while and every now and then he'd feel the end, whittle a bit more, and hold it once again over the flames. When he was satisfied that his work was done and that the tip was hardened properly, he leaned the spear against the tree.

Now he would not be completely defenseless if the wolves returned.

An hour later, as he sat thinking about his situation, it dawned on the old man that he could use the spear to pull the shovel toward him. He stood up, spear in hand, and looked around for the place where the shovel had fallen into the snow. The wind had shaken snow loose from the highest boughs and deposited it all about the base of the tree. Everything looked the same. It was impossible to tell exactly where the shovel lay, so he began poking and prodding the area where he thought it had been, but in his old age, he couldn't remember things too well.

It was his mind, more than anything, that had gotten him into this dangerous situation in the first place. Things weren't clear anymore. Sometimes he couldn't recall what he had done that very morning or what he had eaten for breakfast or lunch. This lack of clarity had crept upon him slowly at first, like a lynx stalking a grouse or rabbit, but in these last years, it had caught up with him and clouded his mind and his judgment. He wouldn't have stepped into his own trap if he had been thinking clearly.

After a while, not having struck the blade of the shovel with the spear, he gave up and sat down again against the tree.

Far, far off in the distance, up higher than any bird ever dreamed of flying, where the air is thin and cold, a jumbo jet was passing overhead. From the great height, even the wide river in the valley below must look as small as the shrew's meandering trail. Least-Weasel watched its white vapor trail for a long time, wondering what the people on board would think of him, so far below, out in the whiteness alone, caught in a trap he had set, chained to a tree, waiting for wolves.

He was tired and it was getting late.

While there was still light, the old man collected more wood from the back of the tree. He broke up smaller pieces over his knee and bigger pieces by standing them up against the tree trunk and kicking them until they snapped. He took these pieces and piled them near the fire to outlast the darkness. The temperature had been dropping all day, and now it was around twenty below. The old man would need the wood during the long night for warmth, for reassuring companionship, as a rescue signal, and to ward off wolves.

One day, a terrible hunting accident happened. The men had been hunting sea lions when a large bull killed the chief. After his potlatch and funeral, the villagers decided to avenge the great chief's death. All the men trained hard. One night, after standing in the sea and beating himself with branches, Blackskin returned to the village, and by the light of the moon, he lifted the great tree right out of the ground! Then, so that no one would know what he had done, he carefully placed it back into the earth.

IT WAS COLD IN THE TINY CABIN when Johnny Least-Weasel awoke in the morning. He had stoked the stove's belly before he went to sleep, but sometime during the night the fire had gone out, and the glowing bed of red embers had turned cool and gray.

He pulled back the heavy blankets. The top was a quilt his grandmother had made for him when he moved into the small cabin close to his uncle's house. The bottom two were cheap blankets given to him at a potlatch when his great-aunt died. In the old times, the tribe had such ceremonies to celebrate life. Nowadays, they only held them when someone died. The dancers used to drink a special cold tea made from a plant called Labrador tea. They had a name for the brew in their language back then, but few elders remember it. Now, after many hours of dancing so hard that the balls of dancers' feet hurt, Pepsi and Coca-Cola were brought out. The last dance used to be in honor of the dancers and the drummers for their hard work. They used to sing one last song as the tea was brought out. Today, they still have such a last song, but it is called the "Soda Pop Song."

Some tribal leaders even tried to pitch an idea to one of the beverage companies for a television commercial. They thought it would sell sodas if a commercial showed a bunch of Indians in traditional regalia dancing to the music of old Indian men drumming and singing in their native language, their feet pounding the floor like thunder. They say that if your feet don't hurt after dancing, you aren't doing it right.

At the end, the camera would focus on a young, good-looking Indian who would hold up a soda can, and the superimposed words *Pepsi—The Official Soft Drink of the Potlatch* would come up on the screen in big letters.

The company never returned the phone calls.

"It's still a good idea," the young man thought, smiling to himself while pulling his pants on both legs at once.

He looked at the thermometer on the wall, the kind that shows both inside and outside temperatures. The cabin was around fifty degrees, which is pretty cold for a house in the morning. It was perhaps five to ten degrees colder at floor level because it was so poorly insulated.

The outside temperature was close to twenty below zero.

Johnny looked out the small front window and wondered about his grandfather.

"He should be home today," he thought.

It was not that he thought his grandfather was weak. Just the opposite. His grandfather was the toughest man he had ever known. Johnny remembered when he had gone moose hunting with him two years before. He had been around fifteen, and his grandfather was in his midseventies, maybe older. They had taken a green flat-bottom boat way upriver and then followed a winding slough back about eight or nine miles. His grandfather knew of a large, partially shallow beaver pond where he had shot many moose over a lifetime of hunting. They camped on a small rise for two days, shot grouse and the occasional duck, and caught fish. One evening, at the edge of dusk, two bull moose stepped out into the weedy pond and began to feed.

Johnny was alone at the time, hiking along the pond's edge in hopes that something would be drawn to the water before it got too dark to see. His grandfather was resting back at camp after an early supper of fish cooked in tinfoil over a campfire.

When Johnny saw the two young bulls emerge from the scraggly forest of spruce and willows, he crouched low to make himself small and crept into the woods, unseen by the moose. When he was certain the moose could not see or hear him, he ran up the trail to camp to tell his grandfather. They gathered what gear they'd need in a pack and tromped back to the edge of the pond. The two moose were still there, standing belly-deep with their long heads submerged, searching for food. They were both spike forks, too young to grow the large palmated antlers of a mature bull.

Two beautiful white tundra swans had come in from the north and landed on the far end of the pond near the beaver dam. It was a beautiful scene—the distant rolling hills, gold and orange with a light dusting of snow on top, the dark blue sky, and the perfect reflection of the swans upon the calm water. A beaver was sitting on the edge of the lake beside his lodge, eating something. It was one of Johnny's favorite memories.

Most people think beavers eat only vegetation, tender branches. But in his lifetime, Johnny had seen beavers eat the heads of salmon lying on riverbanks or on sandbars after the fish had spawned and died in the fall. From a long ways away he had heard their sharp front teeth crunching into the hard fish skulls. Perhaps, he had thought, it was their way of getting calcium or protein. Perhaps they just liked the taste.

His grandfather told him to shoot the closest

moose, which fell on the first shot. The other moose raised its dripping head out of the water, swiveled about its long erect ears, and then, seeing nothing, went back to its meal of pond weeds.

"Shoot that one, too," his grandfather said. "They're small. It takes two this size to make a big one. Shoot!"

After he had shot them both, Johnny and his grandfather waded across the soggy pond, sometimes up to their chests in the freezing, late-fall water, and each took a moose and dragged it back to shore. It was hard work. Though young, each animal easily weighed six or seven hundred pounds. A full-grown bull could weigh up to fifteen hundred pounds. Even more. Some parts of the pond were shallow, only a foot or so deep, and they had to work hard to drag the dead moose over the pond's bottom until they floated again in deeper water.

Once ashore, out of the icy water, they gutted both bulls, dragged the piles away from the work area, and then propped the ribcages open with stout sticks. It was late by then, too dangerous to be working with knives in the dark, so they went back to the camp, built a great fire to dry out their soaked, beaver pond–smelling clothes, and returned the next morning to finish the work after a warm breakfast of oatmeal, hardtack, and steaming hot coffee.

When they were done, each carried loads of almost a hundred pounds of moose strapped to a packboard all the way back to the boat, about a mile below the hill overlooking the pond. On the first trip, Johnny tripped and fell. The pack was so heavy that he could not get up. When his grandfather came back for him, he reached down with one hand and lifted him, pack and all, right off the ground. It took them several trips to haul out all the meat and their camp supplies.

On the way back it rained in great rolling sheets, pouring down from heavy clouds the color of wet gray aluminum, sliding over the earth like a shadow, and within half an hour the silty river itself began to rise.

Johnny could still remember sitting in the middle of the high-sided green boat, facing backward and huddled under a tarp while his grandfather stood at the back of the boat, his hand on the outboard's tiller, with nothing to protect him from the wind and rain. He could still see the cold rainwater flowing down the old man's face, off his nose, and the way he had to squint to see through the rain to read the river's rapid and always-changing channels.

From year to year, the great river was never the same. It's as if such rivers age, grow new lines and wrinkles, sloughs that dead-end, narrow meandering channels half-covered by trees leaning from the steep, fresh-cut banks where their roots will one day give, tossing the tilted trees into the water to be piled up in dangerous logjams downriver.

It must have been around forty above. Maybe a few degrees colder.

It was on that trip that he knew he wanted to be like his grandfather. It was from that experience that he knew his grandfather was the toughest man in the world.

He turned from the cabin's front window, which had a hairline crack running from one side to the other, and rifled through his clothes drawers for a clean shirt. He didn't own many clothes, so the search didn't take long.

Johnny pulled on a yellow smiley-face T-shirt sporting the caption HAVE A NICE DAY! on it, opened the woodstove's door, threw in a couple scoops of sawdust soaked in kerosene, and tossed in a match. When the sawdust was burning evenly, he set two big split logs on top, closed the door, and opened the damper to let the fire breathe.

He was going to work, but he wanted the cabin to be warm when he returned later that afternoon. Johnny closed the door tight, started his snowmobile with one pull after pushing the broken black primer twice, and turned the handlebars and skis toward the village.

There were not many jobs in a village so small. The village centered around a general store with few items on the shelves, where everything cost two or three times what it cost in the larger towns, because the only way to get things this far out from cities in the winter was by the expensive means of small aircraft. Gasoline, diesel, and kerosene, which are mostly barged upriver in summer, cost upward of five dollars a gallon.

The best jobs were usually held by white folks—people working for the state or federal government or who were schoolteachers. Most of the teachers didn't even come from the region. They were often young men and women with a sense of adventure, or they were older folks who'd decided to come out of retirement and go to the far north.

Eventually, though, it didn't matter why they came or where they came from, only that they all left. This harsh land was very different from anything they'd imagined, and the cold and dark and isolation usually got to them in the first six months.

Johnny was a senior with only a few courses left to graduate. He had been taking these classes through a correspondence program ever since the high-school teacher and his wife left the village shortly after the first snowfall. With so much free time, he worked a couple days a week in the general store. It didn't pay much, but it was a job. Besides, the store was an important social place in the community. People came in to buy groceries, gas, and beer. The post office was a little room attached to the store where people could check their mail, too. They always had a coffeepot going, and a CB was hooked up to a car battery so that folks could pass along messages up and down the river valley. Sometimes old people radioed in their grocery orders, and Least-Weasel delivered them on his snowmobile for tips.

When things were slow, Johnny sat at the counter and did his homework. For much of the past year, he had been taking the correspondence courses from the state university. They fulfilled his high-school obligations, but most important, they also earned him college credit. He had never been to the campus, which was far away, but several people he knew had gone there and told him about it. They even showed him photos. Most of them stayed for one semester before the sense of isolation and loneliness brought them back to their village, where everyone was somehow related, where ancestors had lived and died, where the land itself still bore names given to it by Indians.

It was a common story in every village. Grave markers in the many small cemeteries told the stories. It's hard to fit in where you are not wanted and harder still to return to a place that has little future, only a past as old as the land itself. Up and down the great river, in small villages and large villages alike, there were many stories of young people who took their own lives. That's what happens when they stop dreaming; their dreams are washed downriver like ice in the spring.

Johnny had not been to the campus, but he wanted to go there someday—to learn and to get away from the village. His schoolteachers, as transient as they had been, had told him that he was college material. They said he was smart. He went through books the way some people in the village went through beer. He loved great literature and poetry and books about history and art. During the past year, he had used much of the money he earned working at the store to pay for used books and for his correspondence classes. He had finished two courses and was now on his third, a class about American history, including how Columbus sailed to America a long time ago, saw a million Indians already living here, and went back to tell everyone how he had discovered a new world. It was a funny story and all the elders laughed whenever Johnny told it to them.

Sometimes they would come into the store, hang their thick parkas on nails above the stove, pour cups of coffee, and ask Least-Weasel to tell it to them again. It was like hearing a joke everyone knew, including the punch line, but everyone laughed anyhow when they heard it.

"Tell us that story again," they would ask of him while he walked the narrow isles, placing cans and boxes of food into stiff cardboard boxes.

Several of the chapters in Johnny's textbook amused or puzzled or even bothered them. One was about how black slaves, who were stolen from a faraway land, were made citizens who could vote long before Indians could, even though the Indians had lived here for thousands of years and had helped the first white people survive their first harsh winter. Another chapter talked about how many of the first presidents gained office by killing lots of Indians to make way for the land-hungry, expanding nation, as if candidates received votes for every Indian they killed.

Fred Peters came in around noon and asked about Johnny's grandfather.

"Where you grandaddy?" he asked, picking up a box of .22 shells.

Johnny looked up from his book. "He's up on his trapline. Been there for several days now."

The old man placed a package of toilet paper on the counter beside the small green box of rifle shells.

"It been gettin' cold past couple days. He usually come back when it so cold. Not good to be out there alone. Pretty tough be all alone like that."

Least-Weasel was bothered by the old man's words. Fred Peters was only a few years older than his grandfather, and he had quit trapping about ten years earlier. He was a man who knew what trapping was all about, who knew what it meant to be alone and in trouble in the great, unforgiving white.

"I'm sure he'll be home today," he told the old man, collecting his money and giving him his change. "It's only twenty below. I'm sure he'll decide to come home now before it gets colder."

The old man looked outside and then shuffled over to his parka, which was warm now from the rising heat of the stove. "He need to come home today. It gonna get colder. Gonna be real cold tomorrow."

When he closed the door, a little bell jingled, and then it was quiet in the store except for the sound of a log popping in the stove.

During the last half hour before leaving for home, Johnny swept the plywood floor, wondered about his life, about his future, and, most of all, about his grandfather. Although it was only midafternoon, the sun was already heading south.

When he was done for the day, he stopped by to visit his grandmother, hauled in more firewood, emptied her honey bucket down the rough-sawed hole of their outhouse in the backyard, and finally drove home to his own little cabin, which was dark inside and cold again.

Once the cabin was warm, he crawled into his bed, pulled up the blankets and the quilt his grandmother had made for him, and thought about what she had told him.

"You grandaddy should been home today. It gettin' too cold," she had said without looking up from the pot of soup she was stirring on the stove.

Johnny Least-Weasel, warm in his soft bed, a candle glowing on the small table by the frosted window, dreamed all night of his grandfather. They were bad dreams, and he tossed like the icy river tossing in its silty bed.

⚇ *When confronted by the menacing bear, the old*
man wasted no time. He hit the grizzly across
the nose, knocking it over. Then he hit it over the head
until it was dead. The old man had killed a great bear
with only a stick!

IT WAS GETTING LATE, later than the old man usually stayed awake, but he and the night were restless.
Several times he rearranged his bed of green boughs,
pulled the strings tight on his fur-lined parka hood,
turned on his side and tried to sleep. But sleep did not
come. His body was restless and tense from sitting
under the tree all day with nothing to do but worry
and wonder.

It was a perfectly clear night. Frost-sharpened stars

filled the sky; a full moon lit the landscape so bright that he could see across the wide valley; and on the horizon above the far white mountains, the northern lights were shimmering and dancing, pulsing across the sky in long shifting ribbons. The only noise was the creaking of the tree in the wind. He watched the dancing sky for a long time. The shimmering waves of green and red light were beautiful. Words were useless. The borealis must be experienced firsthand to be understood by the heart.

It was a beautiful clear night, even though it was so cold now that his boots and gloves barely kept the old man's feet and hands warm. If the temperature dropped much farther, they would be useless. If there was any consolation in the cold, it was that there were no tormenting clouds of mosquitoes.

He carefully dropped a few more pieces of wood onto the fire, and for a few minutes the flames were happy and provided light and warmth. But no matter how good it felt, the old man knew that there was not enough wood to burn such a bright, hot fire all night. He had to ration what firewood he had, so he curled into a tight ball, hugging himself to keep his body heat from being swept out across the field and into the clear, star-raddled night.

But no matter how tightly he curled up his arms and legs, as if to have them vanish entirely so that the cold could not touch them, he still shivered and trembled. When he opened his eyes, he could see the snowmobile and sled, where his sleeping bag lay inside a dark green waterproof bag.

"How different this night would be curled up in that bag," he thought.

He closed his eyes again and tried to sleep, tried to dream about home and his warm bed in his cabin with its smell of wood smoke and fish-head soup. He tried to dream about his old wife nestled against him in their small, warm bed.

He was close to falling asleep finally when he heard something in the distance. It was getting closer. It sounded like breathing, like panting. Then it was closer, sounding like the panting of sled dogs after a long run. The old man sat up slowly, without turning his eyes from the approaching sound, and reached for his spear leaning beside him.

He could see something coming from the far side

of the field, shadows loping and panting and kicking up snow as they crossed.

Wolves.

He could see them now. There were five. Two were in the lead and three more ran about a body length behind the next. They were coming straight for the tree, straight for the man who did not move or utter a sound.

A lone wolf is a timid creature, nervous and unsure of itself. But a pack of hungry wolves is a dangerous thing, quick and cunning and deadly. The old man remembered how a pack of wolves, scavenging along a great lake, once came upon a cabin with a dozen sled dogs chained to their little windproof houses. The wolves killed and ate several dogs before the trapper, hearing the howling ruckus, came out and drove the wolves away with his rifle. He had had to put down his lead dog.

The wolves stopped when they came upon the snowmobile and its hitched sled, sniffed around for only a minute, until they found the moose quarters. All five attacked, though the frozen meat was not alive and did not move. They ripped the meat from the strings securing it to the sled, dragged it onto the snow, and tore at it and growled and fought one another until there was nothing left but the heavy stripped bones.

Then two of the wolves turned their attention to the huddled shadow crouched beneath the tree. Cautiously, they came closer, weaving from side to side, stopping to look and smell. Curious. Wary.

The others followed.

This wasn't the first time the old man had been encircled by wolves. Once, long ago, when he was still a boy, a pack of wolves had followed him as he trudged home on snowshoes, carrying a rucksack full of rabbits he had shot in the wintered hills. He had been all day in the field with his single-shot .22 rifle. For over a mile they followed him, weaving on and off the trail ahead and behind him. At times, they loped along in the scraggly trees left or right of the trail, hiding behind tree trunks or deadfalls, curious and determined.

When he came upon a clearing, the pack circled him, snarling and snapping at the cold air. He had stood his ground with his rifle, even though he knew he would get off only one shot before the pack fell upon him.

But they didn't.

Both sides stood their ground on that white field, yelling or growling, showing their power and menace. Finally, Albert realized that it was the contents of his pack they wanted. They could smell the game. Slowly,

without taking his eyes off the wolves, he fumbled with the drawstring, opened the bag, reached in and pulled out each rabbit, and flung it as far away as he could. While the hungry pack devoured their easy meal and fought over bits and pieces, the young boy ran home as fast as his snowshoes could carry him across the deep snow.

The wolves did not follow, and he never saw them again.

But on this day, on this wintered field, five wolves were only steps away. The old man stood up and shouted, holding his spear tight in both hands, his legs apart. He yelled and waved the sharp-pointed spear while the wolves growled and bared their fangs and took quick snapping bites out of the cold air, making terrible clicking sounds with their teeth. Their ears were pulled back flat against their dark shaggy heads, and their eyes seemed to glow in the moonlight.

But no matter how loudly the man shouted and no matter how he waved the long spear, they did not retreat. The man's presence might have frightened a lone wolf, or even two, but he did not intimidate a pack of wolves.

Still shouting and holding the spear and without once moving his eyes from the pack, the old man bent over slowly and reached for one of the long, thick spruce boughs he used for his bed. When he found one, he stood up and eased the bushy end into the fire. Within seconds the entire end was engulfed in flames and seemed to light up the whole world. He waved the firebrand, and the wolves, fearing fire more than the old man, turned and ran back into the night, into the trees and on into the far hills.

When he could no longer see them, he placed the burning bough on the fire and stood for a long time, catching his breath and calming his nerves. Somewhere nearby, in a tree across the field, an owl was calling to him. Some Indians thought that the hoot of an owl outside your window at night was a harbinger of death.

But Albert Least-Weasel sat down and did not listen to the owl.

"Go away!" he shouted to the darkness. "Tonight is not my time to die."

His mind began to wander to warm places. He thought about the small sauna behind his cabin. Once a week, he and his wife went out to the sauna and sat inside it until the sweat flowed from their bodies. Every so often, they would step outside to cool down beneath the stars, steam rising off their naked brown bodies.

He wished he could be in the sauna with his wife now.

But there was no warmth here, and no companionship, only a dry wind singing over the snow.

For the rest of the night, the old man did not sleep. He sat with his back to the tree, his arms folded across his chest and his knees tucked up close against his folded arms. He waited like that, watching for shadows to come down from the hill on the other side of the wide moonlit field.

But nothing came.

The hours dragged on, and the night dragged on. Sometime long past midnight, the owl flew away, and the great white world was quiet and empty again, so quiet the old man imagined he could hear starfall as he sat waiting for the onrush of sleep.

▼

THE THIRD DAY

▼

ᛨ *The next day, when the other men approached*
the tree, the very first one was able to wrench it
from the ground. They all shouted, "We are ready!" and
they ran off to their war canoes. Blackskin asked if he
could go, especially since the chief was his uncle. They let
him go, but only to bail water from the back of one of
the long canoes.

JOHNNY LEAST-WEASEL HARDLY SLEPT. The cabin
was warm enough. He even got up in the middle of
the night to toss a few logs onto the fire, but his mind
was full of thoughts about his grandfather. After
lying in bed for hours, he got "Jimmy-legs," a sensation in which his legs felt the need to run, and he
tossed all night trying to make it go away. Johnny was
restless.

When he finally decided to get out of bed in the

morning, it was still dark outside, since the sun didn't come up in winter until almost ten o'clock. It was strange. In the winter, the sun never came up at all in some places, never showed its face even once for more than a month or two at a time. But in the summer, around late June and most of July, it never went down. No wonder they called this place the Land of the Midnight Sun.

And it was.

Johnny made a pot of coffee and read a chapter from his history book and took notes. But every ten minutes or so, he got up and looked at the thermometer. After four or five times, it was clear that the temperature was dropping, only a couple of degrees now, but given several hours it would be perhaps ten or more lower.

It was already close to thirty below.

Had he a telephone, he would have called someone to express his concern for his grandfather. But lacking one, he would have to drive his snowmobile to the village if he wanted to talk.

Johnny put on his heavy winter parka, his white bunny boots—as a generation of soldiers had called the fat white boots—and then his gloves and hat. When he was completely bundled, he went outside to start his snowmobile. But no matter how many times or how hard he pulled on the engine's rope, it would not start. The cold was stronger than his pull, stronger even than his will.

At such temperatures, crankcase oil solidifies and does not pour at all. At sixty below, antifreeze and oil can freeze solid. In the old days, when airplanes were first used in the bush, a pilot would land on a frozen river or a lake or a field, and while the engine oil was still warm, drain the plane's crankcase of oil into a five-gallon tin, which was carried inside and placed near a woodstove. The next morning, the pilot would go outside, brush snow from the wings, check the skis and cables for ice, and pour the warm oil back into the engine. The airplane would start on the first or second try, and moments later the little craft would bounce down the river and take off, flying low above the trees before vanishing in the low sun.

Although airplanes opened the vast expanses of the far north to commerce and trade, it was a rough beginning. Having no knowledge of the science of flight or machinery, many Indians in the early days walked right into spinning propellers and were beheaded.

Johnny went inside to fetch his bucket of kerosene-soaked sawdust and brought out a folded plastic tarp, which he set up over the machine using two saw-horses and a couple logs from the woodpile. Then he started little fires under the tarp, one on each side and close enough to the machine so that the tarp would hold the heat, but not so close that the plastic of the yellow snowmobile or the blue tarp would melt or ignite. He stayed outside for nearly an hour, crouched beneath the tarp to stay warm and to watch the fire. When the flames got too high, he rolled the logs around with a stick.

Close to noon, after the fires had died, he removed the tarp, pumped the primer twice, and pulled the rope's black handle. The engine started on the first pull, sputtered for a few seconds, and then died. He pulled again and again, and finally it started and idled without his working the choke or the throttle.

While the snowmobile was warming, he filled the tank with gas and went inside to wait. He made himself a moose-meat-and-cheese sandwich, cleaned a few dishes, and stoked the stove with a few split logs.

When he looked at the thermometer again, it was thirty-five below.

Johnny drank his last cup of coffee and then drove over to his grandmother's cabin. The ride over was so cold that he had to hunker down below the cracked and duct-taped plastic windshield to keep his cheeks from freezing, so cold that the moisture on his eyes tried to freeze solid, so that, when he blinked, his eyelashes froze together.

When he arrived in the village, little else was moving. All the chimneys poured out smoke, which, because of the cold, settled in the village instead of rising into the clear sky. Even the sled dogs did not come out from inside their little doghouses. They lay curled on straw beds with tails wrapped tightly across their noses, dreaming dog dreams of summer and salmon strips drying on racks in the sun.

From outside his grandparents' cabin, he could see that his grandfather's snowmobile was not out front. Johnny left his machine running while he went inside, afraid that it might not start again.

"*Dzi'di'da*, Johnny," Morrie said.

The greeting was common, though without English equivalent. Loosely translated, it means, "So, you're still alive." In such a dangerous place, where people may not have seen one another for months or seasons at a time, it is not difficult to imagine why this greeting became tradition. It is a salutation that respects survival and resourcefulness.

"Close the door," she said while sweeping the floor.

The young man took off his parka and hung it on a hook near the fire.

"Any word on Grandpa?" he asked.

The old woman stopped sweeping, leaned the battered broom against a wall, and sat down in her chair.

"No," she said finally.

"But, Grandma, it's been too many days and it's very cold. He should have come home when the temperature started to drop."

She didn't say anything, but Johnny could tell that she was worried.

"Maybe he's waiting out the cold in one of his trapping cabins."

His grandmother reached for her sewing things.

"Maybe," she said without looking up.

Johnny sat down on the couch opposite her and rubbed his hands together, trying to warm them.

"Maybe he decided it was better to wait it out."

"Maybe," she said again, but this time she looked up at her grandson and their eyes held, filled with more concern than their words.

They sat quiet for a few minutes. They could hear the clock on the wall, ticking between a picture of Christ on the cross and a print of two wolves lying beside a lake. Their reflection on the still water was that of an Indian man and woman. Husband and wife. Mated for life.

Finally, the old women broke the silence.

"You go look for him, Johnny," she said with a steady voice.

In her Indian way, it was not a request, not a question awaiting an answer. It was a statement, something he had to do, like when she told him to bring in water or firewood.

"But, Grandma, it's almost forty below. Besides, I don't know which cabin he's at."

This was true and the old woman knew it. In her

younger days, she had gone up into the trapline with her husband many times. In the old days, before there were snowmobiles or four-wheelers, they used to go on foot. Back then, it took a whole week to walk in and back out.

"You get you grandaddy," she said again, rising from her chair to check on something cooking on the stove.

"You a good boy, Johnny. You get him."

She didn't say another word after that. When she was done stirring the pot, she walked back into her bedroom and did not come out again.

Johnny checked the woodstove, poked at it a bit with a long iron rod, and then went outside to his still-idling machine. He made a wide turn in the front yard, barely missing several empty fuel drums, and headed back toward the village.

His uncle was working at the tribal office, so Johnny stopped by to talk to him. It was the largest building in the village. It even had a room filled with rows of washers and dryers, which were always broken. Outside, buried under many feet of snow, was a playground built for all the Indian children. But now it, too, was broken. The chains to the swings were gone, and the ladder to the slide was missing. Almost everything was broken in the village—snowmobiles, boats and boat motors, even the village firetruck with its flat tires and the bright red fireweed growing up through its wheels in the summer.

"Come in, Johnny!" his uncle yelled when he saw his nephew.

Even though he drank hard almost every night, his uncle never went to work drunk. It always amazed Johnny that he could do that. The few times Johnny had ever got drunk, he was sick all the next day.

"What's goin' on?" he asked from behind a gray government-surplus desk.

Johnny sat down in the chair on the other side of the desk and looked at the maps on the walls. They all depicted their tribe's land, and each was marked in black ink, denoting Indian allotments and rights-of-way. On the wall behind him was a poster that read "INDIAN POWER" in big red letters and another one with a picture of a bunch of Indian kids that said "INDIAN PRIDE." Posters such as these hung on many walls throughout Indian Country.

"I'm worried about Grandpa," Johnny finally said quietly.

"He's not home yet? I thought he was coming home yesterday."

"No. He's not back. Grandma's worried. She wants me to go get him."

His uncle leaned back in his chair, which creaked from the shifting of his great weight.

"Ah, he's okay. Probably got a girlfriend up there at Twenty Mile."

They both laughed.

Finally, Johnny spoke again. Serious. "I saw Fred Peters at the store yesterday. He thought Grandpa should have come home before the cold set in."

"Tell you what, Johnny. Let's give it a few more days. If he's not back by then, we'll go look for him. Maybe it'll be warmer by then."

Johnny wasn't convinced.

"I don't know. What if it stays cold or gets colder?"

January was the coldest month of the long winter. Sometimes when a cold front came in, it would settle in the valley like a houseguest come to stay too long, and hang around for weeks. A couple of years before, the front stayed under fifty degrees below zero for almost a month before it finally decided to move on to torture villages upriver. At its coldest, it had reached sixty-two below! When the wind kicked up, even a little bit, the temperature was as low as seventy below. At such temperatures, his grandfather would freeze to death within hours if he was not in the warmth and safety of one of his small log cabins.

"Grandpa can take care of himself. He been doin' it for a long time," his uncle said, lowering the front legs of his chair back onto the floor.

Johnny stood up, then looked at his boots while he spoke.

"Maybe I'll go get him today."

"By yourself? You'd just get lost out there. Then we'd have to go look for two people."

Johnny, still looking down, said nothing.

"Don't worry," his uncle said, standing up and escorting his young nephew to the door, one hand on his shoulder. "I can't go now. I have important meetings for the next couple of days. If he's not back by then, we'll go look for him. How's that? It's too late to start today anyway. Besides, don't you have to work at the store?"

His uncle was right on both points. Johnny did have to go to work for a few hours, and it was already getting dark. But darkness really wasn't a problem. It was almost always dark during this time of year, and people traveled up and down the frozen river trails in the dark all the time. His uncle was just using it as an excuse. Johnny didn't really understand why his uncle wasn't more concerned for his own father, but he took his advice to wait.

Johnny went outside to where he'd left his snowmobile idling, zipped up his parka as far as it would go, pulled the strings tight on his hood, hunkered down below the windshield again, and drove to the store. He spent the next four hours sitting behind the counter, reading some of the used magazines on the swap rack because no one came in to buy anything, on account of the cold.

That night he returned to his cabin.

After lighting an oil lamp and starting a fire, Johnny stood outside on the porch for a long time, listening to the slight wind and looking at the frozen river, the stars and constellations, a small square of light cast on the snow from his kitchen window, and the hills brightly illuminated by a full moon.

Next door, he could hear music and yelling and laughing coming from his uncle's house. There was a party again.

The young Indian went back inside his cabin, col-
lected a few of his things, tossing them into a pack. He threw in extra socks, matches, some dried salmon strips, a flashlight, a hatchet, and a sleeping bag. From behind the door he picked up his rifle, a lever-action Winchester with a shoulder strap that was really just a piece of white rope, and checked to make sure it was loaded. Johnny knew that in such cold, as it would surely be the next day, the oil or grease on moving parts of the rifle would become so stiff that the hammer would not fall and the firing pin would not strike the primer to ignite the cartridge. He opened the breach and used cotton swabs and an old handkerchief to wipe away excess oil. When he was done, he put a few extra shells and a small folding knife into one of the deep pockets of his parka.

The next few hours went by slowly. Johnny cooked some dinner—a fried-Spam sandwich—swept his floor, and tried to read his history book. But his mind was preoccupied with thoughts about his grandfather, and he found himself pacing around the cabin like a caged wolf.

Johnny took up his fiddle and sat on the edge of his bed and began to play. The strings were a bit out of tune so he had to adjust them. They were always out of tune, from the constantly changing temperature of the cabin. When they seemed right, he played for a while. His grandfather had taught him how when he was twelve, and he sold several tanned pelts to buy him this violin as a gift. It was perhaps a hundred years old, and it looked it. The flaming on the neck was worn, and there were nicks on the edges of the shoulder and scratches on the face from generations of use. But it had a beautiful deep sound—rich and smooth—and sometimes he and his grandfather played together for hours. Twice a year, they traveled to nearby villages to play with other Indian fiddlers. Those moments were among his happiest memories.

When he was done playing, he carefully placed the fiddle into the old beaten case and sat it back in the corner.

Around midnight, Johnny stoked the woodstove one last time, set his old-fashioned wind-up alarm clock, crawled into his creaking bed with its heavy blankets and quilt, and fell into a fitful sleep.

Outside, beneath the clear light of moon and stars, the temperature dropped, and the thin red line of mercury settled so low in the thermometer that it could barely be seen. It was so cold that the air was stretched tight as a drum.

The small cabins snuggled down into their banks of snow, their windows were dark, and all the people of the village were asleep in their warm beds, shuttered against the cold. Only a little smoke rose from the banked fires. As the galaxy spun around the North Star, bears turned over in their dark winter dens, squirrels burrowed deeper in their nests, and nothing moved on the frozen world.

♦ *After a while, the young men who had run away in fear came back and saw what the old man had done. From then on, those young men respected that old man, who had killed a grizzly bear and taught them a valuable lesson.*

IT IS NOT GOOD TO BE ALONE in the wild when it is so cold, when even thoughts are sluggish and icy.

There comes a point, an irreversible point, from which the body cannot return. It will fight for its right to survive, but in the absence of reprieve, when there is no warm haven, the body will sacrifice bits and pieces, those inconsequential parts that do not heat heart or mind.

The fingers and toes, nose and ears are first to go.

Like soldiers or chess pawns, they are expendable. They buy time for more important functions and organs. At first they hurt, but after a while the pain goes away and you feel warm, falsely believing that the temperature has risen. But they are the false prophets of the North. In truth, those extremities are freezing solid. Blood no longer courses through the veins. It has gone elsewhere. Migrated, like geese or ducks, to a warmer place. Toward the center. The core. It goes there to protect the king, the general, the heart. There, on this small rise, the blood makes its last stand, its defensive effort to purchase the body more time. Once entrenched, it holds the heat close inside and doesn't send it out too far.

The mind no longer sends or receives signals from those faraway places. They are lost continents. Africa. Atlantis. The eyes see the useless hands attached to forearms, tell the brain to make them open things or strike matches, but they do not respond. Cannot. They are no longer of the body. The simplest tasks become impossible.

In such a condition, even if there was a cabin with firewood, kindling, and matches, you might be entirely unable to start a fire. Clumsily, in tears of anger and uselessness, you'd spill the box of matches all over the dark floor. Your fingers would not open or close, having no memory of opposability. At best, you might clutch a match in a fist, press the box against your chest, and in short, deliberate moves, slide the red sulphur head of the match across the rough striking surface. With the hand frozen, you know only by smell if your flesh is burning.

Even assembling the kindling in the woodstove's belly would be a torturous and frustrating exercise. Over and over again you would try to ignite a single match and to settle it properly into the nest of kindling. More than likely, your hand would be unable to pick up a single match, and should it succeed in that simple task, the few matches in the box would likely be wasted before you could carry it in your burning fist to the small pile of tinder. At least you'd die inside a cabin where your body might be found whole and not consumed by wolves or ravens. Eventually, you could be given a proper burial in the late spring after the frozen earth had thawed.

If by miracle you started a fire, the ordeal would not end. Having been frozen so long, without blood circulating to the fingers or toes, they would likely be lost. As the core temperature rises, blood is sent out farther and farther, like a scout. The slowly warming liquid tries to push its way through the frozen veins and flesh. At first, the extremities tingle, like after your hand falls asleep. Shortly thereafter, if you're lucky, the agony arrives, pain so terrible it cannot be explained in words.

The throbbing anguish is for the fortunate. For the unfortunate, the pain does not arrive. Instead, fingers or toes turn black and swell up twice their normal size, burst open and ooze pus. These are called blebs, and they spell the loss of those parts by amputation.

Such loss is common in the Arctic, was common, will always be, and is one of the heavy prices for living on a land so extreme.

Such thoughts filled the mind of Albert Least-Weasel as the cold crept deeper toward his old and brittle bones. He could still wiggle his toes inside his brown leather boots, but his fingers were cold even inside the heavy gloves. Every fifteen minutes, he had to hold them almost into the short flames to warm them so that they would again move properly.

The old man feared that the boots and gloves would be useless if the temperature dropped even five more degrees.

. He looked over at his pile of firewood. It was almost gone. It had gotten him through the shadowy night of the wolves, but he would need more to outlast this day.

Standing up, he saw that he had already broken all the boughs he could reach, except for the one with the squirrel snare on the back side of the tree, and now there was an open area, umbrellalike, where no branches sprouted out from the trunk for almost seven feet. He had jumped a few times to grab the higher branches, but his foot hurt when he landed on the trapped and chained leg, so he stopped trying.

Albert Least-Weasel's stomach growled. His body had burned all of its fuel trying to stay warm, and now he was very hungry. The stomach is a fickle thing. It does not remember the feast it had only days before. It has a very short memory, like a fish that is released only to turn around and bite the same hook a minute later.

If he could only reach up another couple of feet, there would be enough wood. He thought about this until an idea arrived like a small white bird, fluttering around and finally landing in the nest of his mind.

He rummaged through his spruce-bough bed, looking for a particular piece. When he found one that was long and sturdy, he broke off all the small, green limbs leaving only a hook at the end, about a foot long. Maybe a little less. It looked something like a long fish gaff. He raised the hooked end up into the boughs above his reach, hooked the gaff over one of the branches as far away from the trunk as he could, where the bough was thinner and flexible, and pulled down until the end came to within his reach. Then he grabbed the branch as far out as he could, dropped his long pole, and knelt, using his weight and the angle to break the branch clean off the tree in a snap so loud and sharp it sounded like a .22 rifle shot. In summer, the limb would have been flexible, but now, in such cold, it broke easily.

Over the next half hour Least-Weasel was able to break several other long branches from the tree. He snapped off the thin green boughs at the ends and tossed them onto his bed, making it thicker and higher off the ground. The work warmed him so that he unzipped his parka.

A squirrel came out from its tangled nest far up in the tree to investigate the commotion, scrambled down the trunk, its little claws grasping the rough bark, and stopped when it was close above the man. It began to chatter loudly, the way squirrels do when they are angry, shouting at the man to go away.

After resting and eating several handfuls of slush from the fire's edge, the old man began to break the boughs into foot-long pieces. When he was done, the pile was big enough to get him through the short day and hopefully through the night.

Sometime toward light's last breaking, the squirrel scurried down the tree in a loud chatter and scrambled across the lowest branch and into the noose. In a fit of sound and movement, it fell from the limb with the string around its neck and hung itself.

That evening, as stars began to drag across the

arctic sky, Albert Least-Weasel sat beside a warm fire under an umbrella of high spruce boughs holding his skinned dinner on a short stick over the happy flames.

For the last time that day, his stomach growled in anticipation. When his tiny dinner was cooked, he ate it quietly.

For the moment, and perhaps for this moment only, he was content to enjoy the meal and the radiant warmth of the crackling and popping fire. In a different circumstance, he would have enjoyed the quiet solitude, the comforting smell of wood burning, and his small, tasty roasted supper.

After he had eaten, he stood, turned toward his home and his wife, who must be sleeping, and sang his sad love song. He sang it softly at first, but loudly toward the end, as if she might hear it even from this faraway place.

Sometime during the longest night of his life, the ever-hungry wolves came down from the hills again, saw the bright fire burning, heard the old man singing, and turned away back into the dark shadow of the mountain.

THE FOURTH DAY

▼

When they arrived where the sea lions lived, the men took their spears and attacked the great bull, the chief of the Sea Lion People. But every man who tried to fight the bull was killed, and all of the other men ran back to the canoes in fear. Just then, Blackskin walked up to the great sea lion, picked it up over his head, and threw it to the ground. He killed it with his bare hands!

THE NEXT MORNING, Johnny Least-Weasel awoke to the irritating, tinny ringing of his wind-up alarm clock. It was early. Even the sun wouldn't awaken for many hours. It was that interval between night and day when time stops to examine itself.

Before he built a fire or dressed, the young man checked the outside temperature. It was forty degrees below zero. The floor was freezing cold on his bare feet.

Quickly, he built a fire in the stove, dressed, putting

on a heavy red flannel shirt over a white T-shirt and long johns, and went outside to cover the snowmobile with the blue tarp and build fires on either side as he had done the day before.

It was almost two hours before the machine started, but it finally sputtered to life, blowing out a black cloud of smoke in an angry complaint about the cold, then died. It was another fifteen minutes before it started and idled by itself.

While the yellow machine warmed, Johnny refilled the gas tank, checked the blue-black oil level, and strapped an extra can of gas, his pack, and rifle onto the back of the snowmobile. Then he went back inside the warm cabin and waited.

When he was ready, Johnny closed the door tight, pulled his hat down over his ears, pulled his gloves over his hands, and mounted his idling machine. He gunned the throttle and headed out of the village upriver toward his grandfather's trapline.

With sunlight finally rising over the dark-edged horizon, and with his whole body hunkered below the windshield, Least-Weasel sped toward the base of the white hills. With luck, his grandfather would be up there, waiting out the cold in a warm cabin with a pot of hot tea or coffee on the small woodstove, quietly humming one of his favorite old songs that only the elders still knew and sang.

For the first couple of miles after Johnny left the village, a raven flew ahead of him on the trail, landing on one treetop before it would fly on ahead to land and wait on another, as if it were waiting for him, as if it were leading the way. They say that long ago, ravens used to lead hunters to game—caribou and moose— and that in appreciation the hunters shared the remains of the kill, a kind of symbiotic relationship. But over the many generations, both man and bird have forgotten the ancient bond.

After following the frozen river for about fifteen miles, Johnny turned off the well-used main trail, which ran all up and down the great river, connecting many villages, and headed up into the hills. He had been on this trail many times. His grandfather often brought him along to teach him the ways of the hunter and the trapper. Sometimes they came up here in the fall to pick berries and hunt game birds. It was in these hills, almost five years earlier, while picking blueberries and hunting grouse and rabbits in the fall, that Johnny had lost his beloved dog.

Johnny and his dog, inseparable since the latter was a pup, had been hunting in the hills one afternoon. Earlier, his grandmother had made the boy a hot breakfast of pancakes, eggs, and fried Spam, which had been sweetened with a bit of honey drizzled over it as it hissed and sizzled in the cast-iron pan. When she wasn't looking, Johnny had given pieces of pancake to his best friend even though he had just finished his own breakfast of dried dog food mixed with warm water and a few pieces of moose fat trimmed from last night's supper.

After Johnny was done eating and had placed the clean-licked dish in the sink, he put on his shirt and hat and took up his single-shot shotgun, an old 16 gauge his grandfather had given him. He took six shells from a cartridge box on the windowsill and dropped them into one of his shirt pockets. He only needed six. He almost never shot more than two or three birds, but he needed the extra shells because he sometimes missed them on the wing. Though a good shot for his age, the boy had not yet mastered the quick, arcing swing of body and barrel.

Johnny drove a four-wheeler, pulling a small trailer for his dog. The dog sat on a bed of old carpets, watching the village pass as they headed for the trailhead of his grandfather's winter trapline.

The salmon season was past; men were putting up riverboats for the long, dark winter; and sled dogs barked from the roofs of their tiny straw-filled houses. They knew that the putting away of boats meant that winter was coming, and soon the great land would be buried under snow. They would be hitched to sleds and allowed to run and run and run. Sled dogs love to run. They dream of it. All summer they lie beneath the sun, panting and shedding and staring at the sled put away on blocks for the season—tall grass and wildflowers growing up through its runners.

The trail wound its way up into the hills, around small weed-edged ponds, and across a shallow stream. The stream was lined with spruce trees that grew smaller up toward the timberline and with willow bushes and berries. The smell of leaves beginning to decay filled the crisp air. It was perfect country for grouse and moose and bears. After Johnny had parked the four-wheeler, he and his dog walked quietly into the hills, listening to the forest, looking for birds or rabbits, each thinking of what his senses told him or thinking of nothing at all.

Johnny's grandmother was always happy when he brought home a rabbit, but his grandfather was happiest when the boy brought home a porcupine. It was his favorite game meat. The old man would build a fire outside, and when it was hot enough, he would toss the porcupine on the flames, turning it over with a long pole until all the sharp quills burned away, but not enough to cook the flesh. Then he would roll it from the fire and quarter it as he would any other small game. It was an old Indian trick and he knew many others.

Although most of the dogs in the village were malamutes—gaunt, powerful runners—the dog weaving in and out of the forest before the boy was a black Lab, a natural bird dog, named Tikaani. It was the Indian word for *wolf*. The word for *dog* wasn't smooth-sounding and beautiful like the word for *wolf*. Everyone called the dog Tik for short.

All of the other boys, and even many of the elders, made fun of his dog.

"What kind of dog is that?" they'd ask, smiling as they walked around Tik, his tail up and proud.

"Look at him. He's no runner. No good for nothing, just petting. Waste of salmon on him," they'd say.

But Johnny didn't care. He loved the black dog, alone among a village of sleek sled dogs, who were always barking or howling and straining against their ropes or chains.

On the way up to the tree line, Johnny shot a grouse at the edge of a shallow gravel-bottomed creek. The bird had been searching for small stones when the boy and the dog emerged noiselessly from the forest. Tik stood motionless, although his tail twitched in anticipation as Johnny raised the barrel, centered the silver bead sight on the bird, and fired. Within seconds, the dog had jumped across the stream and had the flapping bird cradled in his mouth as he proudly trotted back to the boy, who kneeled and smiled and softly patted the dog's thigh. When the dog dropped the bird at his feet, Johnny rubbed his head and ears, his square head cupped in Johnny's brown hands, and then he reached into a pocket and gave the dog a piece of dried salmon. People called it Indian candy.

Under a bright fall sky Tik followed along with Johnny as he picked blueberries for them to eat. Occasionally, the dog carefully plucked a berry of its own. It was early September and berries at the edge of the timberline were ripe and sweet. Some were as big around as a thumbnail and yet still firm, not soft the way they turn after a freeze. The sun was high, and there was a slight breeze sliding down off the glaciers in the far mountains. It had not rained in a week and few mosquitoes bothered the twelve-year-old and his dog.

The bright hills were orange and yellow and gold and green, and the sky was deep blue with only a hint of thin white clouds strewn in the distance. It was a perfect fall day.

An old army rucksack with the grouse inside sat beneath a tree, while the shotgun leaned against the trunk.

Over the next hour, longer perhaps, they wandered from patch to patch, sometimes simply lying and resting, the sun warm on their skin. Once a rabbit burst from behind a small bush, but the shotgun was too far away.

The two must have fallen asleep, for the boy was awakened by the sound of growling and barking. Startled, Johnny sat up and saw Tikaani growling at a grizzly bear, baring his teeth, the hair on the back of his neck raised like a porcupine. The bear, too, had been eating berries in the hills above the tree line and had stumbled upon the two sleeping friends.

The bear was large, perhaps five or six hundred pounds, his blond head almost two feet across, his dark black eyes set far apart on a flat face. His ears were back, a sure sign of trouble, and he was flashing his yellow teeth, popping his gums, grunting, and shaking his head from side to side.

The young Indian was afraid. He could feel his heart beginning to race, and he had to remind himself to breathe. Slowly, he turned his head toward the direction of the tree where his shotgun rested, but he and Tik had wandered too far away from it. Now the gun was out of sight, forty or fifty yards downhill where they had begun their early afternoon feast.

There's a myth that a bear can outrun a man uphill,

but that a man is faster running downhill. They say it is because the bear's short front legs trip it up. Some books actually advise that you run downhill in such an event. But no matter where you run, up or down or slantwise, you would lose every time. In the hundred-yard dash, a bear can outrun even a horse and take down a moose or caribou or elk. Running is always a last resort, and only when there is some form of safety within a very short distance.

Some books recommend that you jump into a lake or river or stream—suggesting that bears won't follow, that they somehow detest water. Bad advice again. You'll simply end up a wet supper like salmon. Bears are fantastic swimmers.

Some advise that you curl up in a ball and play dead. Do it too soon and you will surely be eaten. Do it only after a foul-breathed bear has knocked you to the ground and begun to claw and bite and rip your scalp away from your head. But if the hungry bear is bent on eating you, fight back with all of your desperate strength, for if you don't, you will surely be killed, partially eaten, and buried for a later meal. Knowing just when to do these things is like playing poker— you have to know when to hold pat and when to call a bluff.

Johnny Least-Weasel knew all these things. He had spent his young life learning the unwritten rules of this untamed land from his uncle and grandfather, and he knew what danger he was in.

He stood up slowly, his eyes on the bear at all times, and he spoke to it, letting it know he wasn't a moose or caribou calf.

The bear saw Johnny as if for the first time. Now it felt outnumbered. Two against one. He charged at the black barking dog between itself and the boy. Out-weighing Tikaani many times over, the bear smashed into him like a furry locomotive, rolling him like a ball tossed into the brush. But the dog jumped to his steady paws and lunged at the bear, barking and snapping, his long tail held high like a flag.

While they battled, their terrible racket echoing in the fall-colored hills, Johnny screamed at the bear, shouting at it, sometimes in English, sometimes in his Indian language. But the bear did not hear or care. It raked its mighty paw at the dog, its dark brown claws almost five inches long. With the grizzly preoccupied, Johnny ran to his shotgun, opened its breech to check that it was loaded, and then ran back to his dog.

The bear was straddled over the Lab, trying to bite his head and neck. But Tikaani was still alive, kicking with his back legs into the belly of the great bear and trying to wriggle free. Johnny took aim and fired one shot just above the bear's massive head. The sharp report echoed in the valley, and the bear bolted toward the tree line.

The boy nervously slid another shell into the breech and walked over to where his dog lay whining and licking his wounds.

Tikaani was breathing fast in short breaths, almost panting. A large section of flesh and muscle was exposed where the bear had torn a length of skin from the dog's back. Small leaves, pine needles, and dirt stuck to the wound. One of his eyes and most of an ear were missing and the side of his head that had taken the mauling was wet and sticky. The end of his long nose was split down the middle and bleeding due to the rake of a huge paw. It was hard to see the red blood against his short, black hair, but it pooled brightly on yellow and orange leaves rotting on the forest floor.

Johnny dropped the shotgun, knelt, put his arms around his dog's head, and began to cry. He held him that way for a long time, and when he let go, Tikaani licked his face.

Still crying, he ran his hand along the length of the dog's body, feeling for what he could not easily see. He found several deep punctures between ribs and scratches that bled when he touched them.

Johnny knew that he had to get help for his dog, but it was many miles back to the small village. Besides, the dog weighed about eighty pounds, maybe more, far too heavy for the boy to carry. But if he left to go for help, surely the bear would return for Tikaani.

So he stayed with his friend throughout the long night. He gathered a great pile of dry branches and built a fire close enough to the dog to warm him. As darkness fell and stars and constellations came out, he cleaned the grouse and roasted it on a stout green stick over the flames. Johnny offered his dog bits of the meal, but in such pain as he suffered, Tikaani would not eat. Johnny ate the grouse, and when he was done, he collected pitch from a nearby spruce tree, which he chewed until it was warm and soft, then rubbed it into the many wounds and cuts. It was old Indian medicine his grandmother had taught him.

As the night grew cold, Johnny laid the empty rucksack, like a canvas blanket, over the dog. Occasionally, through the blackness beyond the edge of the campfire's glow, came the sound of snapping branches, as if something was moving through the night, circling, kept at bay by the fire.

The boy passed the long night with his shotgun on his lap, tending to the fire and caressing his dog. But somewhere before light's first breaking, he fell asleep with one arm wrapped across his friend.

Johnny was awakened by the voice of his grandfather, calling his name and shaking the cold from his bones. But his dog never woke again.

On a crisp fall morning, Johnny Least-Weasel, then but a twelve-year-old boy, buried his best friend just above the timberline and marked the shallow, knife-hewn grave with a pile of stones.

The stone pile lay somewhere ahead on the trail, like a milepost.

Although it had not snowed in the village for some time, it had recently snowed in the hills as it almost always does when low winter clouds become tangled in the mountains.

Johnny drove his yellow machine up the trail, snow sometimes billowing over the engine cowling, and it bothered him that there were no tracks of any kind on the virgin snow. It meant that his grandfather had not come down, that he was still up there somewhere, alone. Although the snow was fairly deep, the machine pressed on, riding lightly on its wide tracks and skis.

The sun was about as high as it would get at this time of the year. There would be only a few good hours of useful light before dusk.

Rounding a bend, two white rabbits quickly hopped across the trail and vanished in a thick tangle of spindly spruce. They wouldn't usually come out from their burrows when it was so cold, but the noise of the machine winding its way through the stunted forest startled them.

Johnny's cheeks were cold and his nose was running. He stopped, took off his gloves, and stood on the idling machine's runner while he cleared his nose, pressing his index finger against each nostril and blowing hard onto the snow. He checked that his gear was securely strapped, then sat and rubbed his cheeks until they felt warm again. After sliding his hands back into the sealskin gloves, he gunned the throttle, and the machine resumed its uphill trek into the white hills.

Less than a mile farther on, he came to a fork in the trail. He knew this place well, where his grandfather's trapline took two different routes, one winding far back into a remote valley, the other equally far into another. A small log cabin, some twenty miles distant, marked the end of each trail. Each cabin was only twelve feet by twelve feet, with one window in the front by a heavy door. Inside each cabin was a bunk bed, one small table with two mismatched chairs, an oil lamp, and a woodstove made from an old fifty-five-gallon fuel drum with a hole cut in the back for the insertion of stovepipe. There were no pictures, but one cabin had an old faded calendar that had been tacked to the wall in 1963. It had a sketched picture of a new Chevrolet parked before a new brick house, with a beautiful woman wearing a red dress and a shiny black belt standing beside the car.

The blank surface of snow gave no hint about which way Johnny should go. Both trails lay equally white and undisturbed. It reminded him of a poem he had read. One trail would take him to his grandfather, the other would not. It was that simple. It would take almost two hours to drive back to the end of either of the two trails, and it would take only a little less coming back, to return to this fork, by which time it would certainly be dark. If the old man was waiting warm and safe in either of the cabins, it would not matter which trail he took at this moment. But if his grandfather was in trouble . . .

With worry tight as a fist in the pit of his stomach, Johnny Least-Weasel said a small prayer, to whom or what he did not know, leaned forward behind the windshield, and took the left trail. At every turn, he hoped that he'd find his grandfather rounding a bend on his way down. But every turn was the same—white, unbroken, silent, and lonely—so he kept going, kept hoping that he would find the old man at his cabin with a plume of gray smoke rising from the chimney.

After several miles of winding up into the tortured landscape, Johnny came upon an opening in the forest of spruce and snow. It was a small lake, really more marsh than lake, perhaps only several hundred yards across. It was fed by a warm underground spring, and its surface was only partially frozen in the middle. There, the water was deep, and heated bubbles rose from the pressured depths of the earth. A layer of snow lay upon the surface, and the young man was unaware of the danger beneath it.

Johnny aimed his machine for the far side and raced across the marsh as fast as the snowmobile could go, its high-pitched engine screaming and kicking up slush and water and ice. Less than halfway across, Johnny realized his mistake, but it was too late to turn back or slow down. All he could do was lean back on the machine to keep the heavy engine and skis from diving in, hold the throttle down as far as it would go, and pray that it would not stall or run out of gas before he reached the other side. If he fell into the water, he would surely die within an hour.

The snowmobile slowed and rocked sluggishly as the rear sank into the darkness, but the wide track kept turning and turning, swimming its way toward the far bank. Then, close to shore, where the lake was shallow and weedy and where snow turned to ice, the straining machine and its nervous cargo rose out of the water and slid on its metal belly into the scraggly trees of the white, frozen forest.

A raven sitting atop a small tree watched, then flew away cawing loudly.

Sometime after noon, Johnny reached his grand-father's trapping cabin. There were no tracks in the snow, no snowmobile, no gray smoke billowing from the rusted chimney stack, and no grandfather.

He had taken the wrong trail.

Now, there would be only enough light to return to the fork. It would be dusk, even dark, by the time he'd set off up the other trail. Perhaps by then, he hoped, he'd find snowmobile tracks on it and he'd know that the old man had come down out of the hills and was on his way home.

Johnny made a tight circle in the small clearing around the cabin and saw that his gas-tank gauge was already below the halfway mark. The deep snow had slowed his ascent, caused him to burn more fuel than he'd expected. But going back would be faster. There would be his freshly broken trail, and it was downhill all the way. Anxiously making a quick calculation, Johnny determined that he had enough gas left in the tank to return to the fork and explore only the first few miles of the other trail. After that, he would have to use the extra fuel in the gas can strapped to the back of his snowmobile to return home.

As gravity pulled him down the mountain, ten miles an hour faster than he had come up, Johnny could only hope that his grandfather was safe inside the other cabin with a warm blazing fire and plenty of firewood stacked on the small covered porch. He was angry with his uncle for convincing him to wait so long and mad at himself for not being strong enough to go anyhow. He loved his uncle, but sometimes he did not understand him.

Burning daylight is a common northland phrase that refers to the shortness of days, and that's just what Johnny was doing now as he gripped the handlebars tightly, leaned into sharp turns, and raced against the sun. He braked only twice the whole way down to the fork, leaned close behind the windshield, and raced against time.

The other men were amazed and impressed. They had never seen such courage and strength in a man. When they returned to the village, Blackskin was made chief. He used his power only for good. He was truly a great man.

THE NIGHT WAS SO LONG it seemed as though the sun might never rise again. After so many hours, the old man began to think it was too cold even for the sun. He imagined it huddled somewhere, waiting for the white world to warm up before it would return from its sleeping place somewhere far, far below the earth's easy curve.

For the most part, the dark had been silent and uneventful. Because of his pile of wood, he had been able to keep his fire burning, and because he had tossed the extra boughs onto his bed, the frozen ground was unable to steal the warmth from his trembling body. The freezing air, though, took as much as it wanted.

And it wanted everything.

In order to pass the night, the old man clung to his routine. He'd toss a few pieces of wood onto the fire, make sure it caught, and then sleep uncomfortably for maybe half an hour. He'd awaken, toss more wood onto the glowing bed of embers, watch and listen to the shadowy hills, and then he'd sleep again, his whole body trembling, his teeth chattering. Sometime during the night, the curious wolves came down but left without event. And sometime toward the end of the night, it became clear that his supply of firewood would not last. Keeping the flames warm and bright throughout the never-ending dark came at a price, and the old man found himself at a crossroads.

On the one hand, the small pile of firewood was running low and would be consumed, no doubt, in the next hour or two. To conserve his precious fuel, he further rationed it, but by doing so, the fire gave off too little heat, not enough to warm him even if he crowded it with his hands. On the other hand, he had his thick bed of spruce boughs. The pile kept him off the ground when he slept, but if he slept now, he knew that he might never awake.

Finally, the flame of dawn lifted over the mountaintops, and morning came into the huddled valley.

The old man's pile of wood was gone. He had survived the night, but to what end? Now he would have to face the day. The temperature had plummeted to around forty-five below. At such temperatures, the day is little warmer than the night. He had been in colder. Once, when he was a young man, the temperature was seventy degrees below zero. In such tremendous cold, the moisture in breath freezes instantly and falls to the ground like salt.

His one real choice was to burn his bed, keep a big fire so that the freezing would not go too deep into his old bones. Looking at the bed of boughs, most branches at least six feet long, he figured that he'd make it until noon. After that, nothing would save him. He would freeze and die, and someone would find him chained and frozen to this tree. Perhaps the lack of branches on the tree and the sturdy spear would tell them that he had made a good stand, that he had fought as long as any man could have fought, that he had missed nothing, forgotten nothing, that he had used everything, every resource and lesson, but that in the end, even the greatest grizzly bear cannot defeat winter.

But the old man knew better. He knew that without the fire the wolves would return, find him frozen like the moose hindquarters on the sled, and that they would fight over bits and pieces until there would be little for his son and grandson to find when they came into these hills in search of him after the cold had moved out of the valley.

Around noon, his fire gone save a glowing mound of embers and the very small ends and bits of twigs, the old man sat with his back against the tree, much as he had done for the past days, but now he had nothing to insulate him from the ground. He was very cold, and he huddled and tried to keep his body heat close. There would be no more fire, no more reprieve from winter. Finally, he was at his end. All living things must come to this lonely moment. Even the wolves that would no doubt fall upon him this very day, this night for certain, would in the next few years meet their own ends as well. The tiny shrew whose tracks encircled the tree would meet its end, most likely by the owl that called his name every night and that one day would wake and fly no more, and end. The irritated squirrel had already met its end. So, too, had the moose he had killed up the trail. The end came to everything that lived. Especially in these white hills where the circle of life was undisturbed, like the deep snow on the field.

And it would come to Albert Least-Weasel too.

Halfway toward a worried and dark sleep—sitting with his back to the tree, arms wrapped around himself and chin resting on his knees, his hood pulled tightly closed—he became aware of a sound, almost nothing at first. The old man felt himself wonder if this was the sound of his ending, a sound wolves and shrews and owls also hear at their ending, a kind of universal sound in the ears of all living things. But after a minute he looked up, pulled his hood back, cocked his head, and listened hard outside himself, above the sound of a slight breeze and his own breathing.

It was the unmistakable sound of a snowmobile far away. It was coming up into the hills. He turned his ear toward the sound, downhill, and strained to listen. Someone was coming. On this coldest day of the year, someone had left the village to come find him. The old man struggled to unbend himself and stand, to look down the trail as far as he could. His old body ached.

But then the sound dropped to a lower, more consistent level. It was so low that the wind blew it away like a brittle leaf barely hanging from a limb. He could still hear it when the wind let up, but it didn't seem to be moving. He knew where it was. It was at the fork less than two miles away. He imagined the driver trying to decide which trail to take. Left or right. One valley or the other. After a minute, the sound became louder, was on the move again, and it seemed to be coming toward him. But a short time later, the sound seemed to be moving in a different direction, away from him.

The diminishing sound was now going in the wrong direction. It had been an even chance to pick the trail that led to this tree, but even fate, it seemed, was against his rescue.

Least-Weasel listened to it fade off into the next valley. Then he stirred up the remains of the fire with his heel until he could see red beneath the grayish ash. He bent over and pushed his hands into the ashes and found some sense of warmth nestled at the heart. Even this little heat would soon be gone. The old man hunkered over the dying heat until the remnants that held it turned gray and cold. He figured it would take a good three or four hours before the snowmobile would return to the fork and begin to search this valley.

He had only to survive that long.

But it would be difficult without fire or shelter, and his reckoning, in the afterglow of his earlier elation, was that the challenge was beyond the capacities of his aged and unwilling body. His hands were fine for now, but he had not been able to feel his toes for the better part of the day, and he had trembled mightily during the last hours before dawn. With so much of his energy already lost, he had little strength remaining with which to put up a long, hard struggle. "Heroism is the task of the young," he thought. Life is precious, but wolf or man, young or old, everything that breathes must, finally, accept the end. It is not simply the Law of Nature, it is the one common thread that binds all living things. Even the tallest trees in the forest, hundreds of years old, will one day reach up to the sun no more.

The old man sat back against the trunk and huddled again and closed his eyes. A strange memory came to him, one he'd not thought about for decades. Some thirty years before, one of the men from the village went up to his trapline. When he didn't return after a week, his relatives went looking for him. But they did not find him. More men from a village upriver joined them because his wife was from there, but he was never found. A few years later, Least-Weasel was hunting in that area and found a skeleton under a tree far from the main trail. It was white and dry and picked clean. Many of the longer bones were missing, but the skull remained, and there was a badly rusted rifle still leaning against the tree. It had the initials of the owner carved into the stock.

Albert Least-Weasel, then a much younger man, took the skull and the rifle back to the village, and the sons of that man knew that these things belonged to their father. For whatever reason, they nailed the white skull to the top of their meat cache, a small log house on tall legs, usually raised about seven or eight feet off the ground so that animals cannot steal its contents of dried meat or fish. Almost a year later, the largest grizzly bear they had ever seen stepped from the leafy forest, stood on its hind legs, and rocked that cache until it toppled, spilling its store of moose and salmon. The great bear ignored the food, and, taking only the skull, gingerly tucked it between his yellow teeth and padded quietly back into the forest.

No one really knows why it happened or what it meant, only that it did happen. Perhaps the man's spirit became that bear and simply reclaimed what was rightfully his. The family still had an old black-and-white photograph of the skull nailed atop the cache to prove the story was not myth or legend.

The man wondered what story they would tell about him. Would it be a tale of courage and strength or one of foolishness in old age?

For the next hour or two, the only things that moved were a lone raven and the man's huddled shadow slowly following the tree's as the low sun rounded the curve on its ancient path. The breeze came suddenly in small gusts and carried away the ashes of the fire like powdery gray snowflakes, until there was only a dark hole where the fire had burned itself into the ground, like a sled dog digging into the snow to hide from the wind.

The old man's snowmobile and sled full of gear, including the protruding ax handle, sat quietly. Sometimes he thought he could hear the wind carrying the song of the ax, singing the way it does when it splits spruce or birch. But it was only a lonely raven cawing out in search of any other living thing. It did not look on the man as living. It knew what the tree had known for some time, knew what the wolves in the bright hills knew as they came down through the scraggly forest, over deadfalls, toward the wide field of deep snow and the old man freezing and chained to a tree.

He could see them far up in the valley, at the timberline, coming down, weaving in and out, and passing one another, sometimes in formation like geese. They were coming to him, and this time he would offer little fight, like a week-old calf or a very old moose or caribou that cannot run.

For the first time, a thought arose in his mind that he would never again see his home or his wife. And the thought made him sad.

Then, softly at first, softer than the ax's singing, he heard something. It came only for a second, then vanished, and then came again, until it was constant and droning.

It was the snowmobile. It had gone to the end of the trail, found only the untracked white emptiness, and was returning to the fork. It would arrive upon this field within minutes, but by then it might be too late.

The old man looked up the valley, saw the gray-coated wolves coming, studied the speed of their graceful, loping descent, turned his ear toward the sound of the snowmobile and judged its speed. It would be close, he thought, so he gathered his remaining strength and slowly stood up. He felt as cold and brittle as an icicle. He rubbed his thighs and felt nothing. They were frozen. He tried to move, but his legs would not do as they were told. So he stood there, teetering, trying to steady himself. He reached for the spear, but his hands could not grasp it. His fingers would not open or close, so he hooked it in the crook of his arm, cradled it under his right arm against his ribs as tight as he could, and let the spear lie loose across his left forearm close to the wrist.

He would fight. No matter that it was his time, he would at least make the wolves work for their meal, the way all things, even when old or crippled, struggle for survival.

They were close now, already at the far end of the field, emerging like gray ghosts from the trees. They were coming fast, determined, and their eyes saw only the tree and the man and the wide distance between.

On the other side of the field, much farther away than the pack, a yellow snowmobile emerged from the tree line, its dim headlight bouncing in the fading light of dusk.

Albert Least-Weasel stood as tall as he could, like a small animal trying to look big. He pressed the pole as tightly as he could against his side, and though he could not feel the pressure, he knew that the spear was snug and that it would not easily be knocked loose from its hold. He turned up his wrist so that his frozen hand made a kind of rest for the front of the spear, turned himself toward the wolves, crouched slightly for leverage and balance, and held his breath until there was no sound in the world but the rapid beating of his heart and the quick panting of wolves.

In a wide field of deep snow, in the white rolling hills above a great winding river somewhere in the far north, an old man waited while time slowed, while the very speed of light slowed, until there was nothing but time and no time at all and a snowmobile and a tree and hungry gray wolves, and an old man holding his breath and waiting.

From the tree line on the riverward side of the field, Johnny stood, squinting above the windshield. Far-away, he could see his grandfather's snowmobile and the dark shape of a man standing beneath a great tree, and a pack of wolves springing through deep snow toward him.

Their approach wasn't cautious, as it had been before. They knew that there was little fight left in the old man. This time they went straight at him, biting and ripping and clawing. Johnny couldn't make his machine travel any faster, and though he was still too far away, he began to yell at the top of his freezing lungs while the flat white distance between them closed.

The sound of the distant machine and the screams of curses meant nothing to the wolves as they closed on the old man in a tight, vicious circle. Their snarling and growling, together with the terrible clanking of the chain as the old man punched and kicked and stabbed with his now-broken pole in his frantic struggle for life, drowned out the sound of the rescuer's approach.

Johnny pulled up behind his grandfather's machine and sled. Without turning off the engine, he jumped from the machine, pulled his rifle from its scabbard, quickly worked the lever action in one swift motion while stepping toward the tree, and fired into the crisp winter air. The first shot startled only one wolf, which turned and flashed its teeth. But the others did not stop their attack. Johnny stepped closer and fired again. This time they all stopped, turned around and saw the man, heard the idling snowmobile for the first time and the angry words of the man calling to them. They smelled gunpowder and steel.

When the young Indian shot into the air yet again, they ran away, back up into the white hills from where they had come—back up to where the moon sat on the clean-lined edge of a steep ridge.

Johnny ran through the deep snow to his grandfather, who had fallen backward into a half-seated, half-lying position. He leaned his rifle against the great tree and spoke to him.

"Are you all right, Grandfather?" he asked.

The old man looked up into the face of his desperate grandson, nodded slowly, and said nothing. His parka sleeves and his pants were ripped and his hands and arms were bleeding.

Johnny saw the trap and the chain bolted to the tree. Instantly, he understood why the old man had not returned to the village. He ran back to his snowmobile, grabbed his sleeping bag, and seized the long-handled ax from his grandfather's sled. Returning, he knelt beside the wounded figure and wrapped him snugly in the sleeping bag. The old Indian leaned forward, making himself small within the warming layers.

While his grandfather rested and warmed, Johnny studied the trap. In fighting off the wolves, the sharp, metal teeth had worked their way through the boot leather and insulation into flesh and bone. Johnny was concerned about releasing the tight-springed trap, that doing so might do more harm than good, so he decided to leave it on until they reached the village.

Instead, the young man hacked into the frozen trunk of the tree around the steadfast, rusted bolt, while the old man, still and huddled within the wrapped sleeping bag, watched the sun's quiet descent, saw its distant burning on the edge of the frozen world before it disappeared.

Johnny heard something in between swings of the ax. It was very faint. Almost imperceptible. He stopped for a moment to listen. It was the old man singing a song in their Indian language. The young man leaned closer so that he could hear. He recognized the song even though he did not know the words. He listened until a cold gust of wind reminded him of his burden, and he went back to work on the unyielding tree.

Within minutes the bolt fell free.

"Hold on," he said to his grandfather while he rushed to clear the sled and hitch it to his own machine. He found his grandfather's sleeping bag among his survival gear and quickly unrolled it inside the belly of the sled, which would now serve as a stretcher. Then, with the engine stopped for safety, he poured the extra fuel into the gas tank, almost filling it.

The building silence was deep but not comforting. Now Johnny could hear the quietness of the field and his own rapid breathing. The tightness in his throat made the sound louder than it should have been.

Then he went to his grandfather to carry him to the sled, but the old man did not look up from beneath his blanket wrap. He sat still and quiet below a ceiling of spruce trees and stars, bent over, head drooped.

He would not speak or sing again.

Somewhere, high up in the branches above, Johnny heard an owl.

He sat with his arms around his grandfather. His breathing had become inaudible and the world was quiet and peaceful and beautiful. Johnny sat and cried for a long time in the freezing darkness with his arms around the old man, feeling sad and angry and guilty that he had not listened to his own heart. He should have come days ago. He knew that the land was dangerous and that danger comes quickly, all of a sudden, like an avalanche or a flash flood. Now the mountain had taken two lives from his life. He could blame the cold and the wolves, but he also blamed himself.

When he was done crying, Johnny stood up, wiped his face with a parka sleeve, and used the ax handle for leverage to release the trap's deep bite, pulling the old man's mangled foot from its grip. He dragged his grandfather over to the snowmobile and carefully placed him on the sled, covered his body with the sleeping bag, and secured him with rope. Then he stood in the quiet field looking around him. He saw a raven sitting on a faraway tree and the wolves standing on a moonlit ridge, watching him. He looked down at his grandfather, saw how small he looked now, a man who had been so strong in life. He thought about life in the village, how the place was like a trap, its sharp teeth forged from the fire of two worlds colliding.

His mind filled with thoughts, Johnny pulled his thick gloves over his cold hands, raised his fur-lined hood over his head, and yanked the starter rope hard. The machine sputtered to life, belching blue-black smoke as it made a broad turn in the somber field. With only light from the moon and a dim headlight as guides, he slowly descended from the white hills, down toward the wide, sleeping river, and home.

And the silence of the land moved with him.

GOFISH

JOHN SMELCER

What did you want to be when you grew up?
At first, I wanted to be a military officer like my father, but I quickly learned that what I really wanted was to be a teacher. I've taught college literature and writing for the past eighteen years.

When did you realize you wanted to be a writer?
My mom says I was writing and illustrating little books when I was just six or seven. I didn't really start writing until my late twenties, and then mostly poetry. I didn't try my hand at fiction until I was forty.

What was your worst subject in school?
This is funny: English. I remember my high school English teacher saw me one day after I'd earned my degree in English and education. She couldn't believe that I majored in English. She said I was one of her worst students.

Where do you write your books?
That's really changed over the years. At first it was always at my desk in the den and always, always at night after my wife and daughter settled down for the evening. I've written the last three books at coffeehouses on a laptop.

When you finish a book, who reads it first?
My friend Bard Young, who lives 3,000 miles away in Tennessee, is the first person to read any book I write. I value his feedback more than anyone else.

Which do you like more, cats or dogs?
For ten years my family had two cats and two dogs. I always thought of the cats as my wife's pets; the dogs were mine. In fact, the dogs, Tik and Sagan, went everywhere with me, sitting up front in my pickup truck.

Where do you go to find peace and quiet?
I have a beautiful cabin on a river about a hundred miles north of where I live outside Anchorage, Alaska. The cabin is in a neat little town called Talkeetna. Whenever I'm pretty much finished writing a book, I print the whole thing, bind it, and take it to the cabin for several days of editing and relaxing in the local cafes.

What are you most afraid of?
I know this sounds bad for a grown man to say, but I fear loneliness the most. I don't know why, but I don't like to be alone too long.

Which of your characters is most like you?
I am Johnny from *The Trap*. Notice my name is John. I created him from my own life experiences.

What is your favorite TV show?
I've always loved *M*A*S*H*. It just makes me happy.

If you were stranded on a desert island, who would you take for company?
This is easy: my wife. She's my best friend.

What do you consider to be your greatest accomplishment?
I get this question all the time, and people expect me to name one of my thirty books. But the truth is, I'm most proud of my family; of having been a good father and husband.

Who is your favorite singer?
Elvis Presley. His first name is tattooed on my right shoulder.